# COURTING SPARKS

Other books by Joselyn Vaughn:

*CEOs Don't Cry*

# COURTING SPARKS

•

## Joselyn Vaughn

*AVALON BOOKS*
NEW YORK

Published by Avalon Books,
an imprint of Thomas Bouregy & Co., Inc.
160 Madison Avenue, New York, NY 10016

Library of Congress Cataloging-in-Publication Data

Vaughn, Joselyn.
    Courting sparks / Joselyn Vaughn.
        p. cm.
    ISBN 978-0-8034-7702-5
    I. Title.
    PS3622.A953C68 2010
    813'.6—dc22
                        2010022410

PRINTED IN THE UNITED STATES OF AMERICA
ON ACID-FREE PAPER
BY HADDON CRAFTSMEN, BLOOMSBURG, PENNSYLVANIA

For Joe

*Acknowledgments*

Special thanks to Wendy, Theresa, Marianne, and turkey artichoke sandwiches.

## Chapter One

*Sandalwood and a touch of woodsmoke.*

The scents drifted from behind her, and Daphne knew the man was sexy. She closed her eyes as she stood on the corner of the dance floor and breathed deeply. Maybe passing out candy bars for the Dollar Dance wasn't such a bad thing. Her Magic Eight Ball could be right. For once.

She tried to adjust the neckline of her fuchsia bridesmaid dress to enhance her cleavage, but the double-sided tape holding the mermaid-style dress in place wouldn't budge.

Sure, when you want the dress to come off, it sticks firmly in place. She sighed. She spun on her bare feet to greet the dream date behind her and stopped so abruptly, her basket of candy bars tipped over, spilling chocolate at his feet.

"Noah?" she gasped.

A light blue madras shirt covered his broad shoulders. His dark hair was still damp from his shower. She looked at him like she'd never seen him before.

Yet she saw him almost every day. He was the athletic director and she was an English teacher and the cross-country coach. She was in and out of his office with student eligibility reports and questions about the team schedule. Besides all that, they'd been friends since second grade. She'd never had this reaction to him before. What was different?

1

Noah bent to pick up the candy. His shirt pulled across his muscular shoulders as he reached for the scattered bars. Daphne continued to stare at him. Water droplets clung to the hair on the back of his neck and she itched to brush them away. She extended the basket for him to dump the chocolate.

"Fire call?" she said, trying to cover her stunned silence and hoping he didn't notice her blushed skin.

"Yeah. Out at the Willows. Could have been really bad, but we were able to contain it. Do I still smell smoky?"

Daphne leaned closer and breathed deeply. His sandalwood cologne flooded her nose again. A touch of smoke lingered behind it. She forgot to breathe out.

This was Noah, she told herself. Not George Clooney. *Get a grip.*

"Your cologne covers it. How much burned?" she asked, stepping away to put some fresh air between them.

Noah shrugged. "The flames kept smoldering in this heat. Hot spots were flaring up all afternoon. Most of the trees are singed. I'm not sure they'll come back." He tugged at the front of his shirt as if he still felt the high temperatures.

"I can't believe the Willows is gone. No more hidden trysts out there. Where will the teens go to make out now?"

"They'll find someplace. They always do. There's that place by the river, but the landowner is pretty adamant about kicking them out once a month."

She hugged the candy basket to her chest. Bittersweet memories of the Willows haunted her, now that Aaron was no longer in her life. They'd gone there to do all the things teens do in the shaded alcoves of the draping willow trees. The fire was a relief in a way, another reminder of him gone.

"Was Miranda angry I wasn't here?" Noah asked.

She glanced at the bride twirling on the dance floor and pushed away the gloomy thoughts. *Good ol' Noah.* He could always divert her depressing thoughts. "I think she'll forgive you." Daphne bumped him with her basket of chocolate. "Not to dash your ego, but she didn't notice. She was so nervous before the ceremony, she peed every fifteen minutes. I'm glad I didn't pull bathroom duty this time."

Noah laughed, the tone soft and deep. "I don't want to know. Anything else happen?"

"If you're asking if Max fainted, you owe me ten bucks. He turned green during the solo, but his knees never buckled." She nodded in Max's direction. He was dancing something barely recognizable as the Twist with his grandmother.

"I thought I had a sure thing on that one. How many bets have you won now?"

"I'm up eighteen to one on the weddings. You haven't won since you guessed Brent and Missy would have Warren six months after the ceremony. I still think you had insider information."

"I'll never tell." Noah shook his head and dug into his back pocket for his wallet. He fished out a ten-dollar bill. He waved it in front of her face. "Double or nothing for Jake and Beth's?"

Daphne snatched the bill and instinctively reached for a pocket. "As ugly as they make these dresses, something as functional as a pocket wouldn't ruin it," she muttered, as she folded the bill and tucked it into the bodice. It caught on the tape. At least she wouldn't have to worry about losing it.

She noticed Noah's gaze follow her hand and linger there. Her fingers trembled. She turned her shoulder to him and shoved the bill down into her bra. When she looked up, he was surveying the dance floor. No, she must have imagined his look. Guests mingled around the gazebo and under Chinese lanterns that gave the growing twilight a warm glow. Suitably dreamy for a wedding.

"I don't see either of them fainting, and Beth has every detail nailed down. Her only snafu is that the bridesmaids' dresses haven't arrived yet."

He pursed his lips, thinking. "I bet they won't fit."

Daphne rolled her eyes. "You can't bet on that. There's always something wrong with the dresses. That's like betting Coach Reynolds'll be a jerk. It's a sure thing. The lady in the shop has taken my measurements at least four times and my dresses still don't fit. They had to tape me into this Mermaid Barbie monstrosity."

The switch bell chimed and a new song started up. It was Noah's turn to dance with Miranda, but he waved the person behind him onto the dance floor. Daphne tried to ignore the flood of relief that he wasn't leaving her. She hated standing here while inebriated relatives queued up to dance with the bride and groom. It was just another bridesmaid duty she couldn't shirk.

"We have to bet on something," Noah said. "It's the only thing keeping me awake through the ceremonies."

"Whether Aaron will show up?" Daphne offered him a fake grin. She thought she saw the fine lines around his eyes tighten. "He claimed Jake was his best friend. After his favorite cousin, of course."

Noah rolled his eyes. "Favorite cousin when he needs cash. He called you again, didn't he?"

She nodded. The cold, queasy ball in her stomach sank just thinking about it.

"Why won't he let you go?" Noah muttered under his breath. He balled his fingers into fists. "It's like he doesn't want to be with you, but he doesn't want to give you up either."

"Something like that." She shrugged. "He doesn't want to give up the best years of his life. When we were together, he was the star quarterback and I was the homecoming queen. I don't think his current life has as much grandeur."

Noah tilted his head closer and a wave of his cologne flooded over her. He briefly squeezed her bare shoulders. Daphne felt herself leaning into him, relishing the security and understanding she always found in him.

"You want to do this someday?" He nodded his head toward the bride dancing ring-around-the-rosy with two young girls. They must have gotten to "we all fall down" because the two girls dropped on their behinds, kicking their feet in the air. Miranda saved her white dress from dusting the floor by squatting down and clapping her hands.

"I think my ring-around-the-rosy days are well behind me." She sifted through her basket of candy, pulled out a 3 Musketeers, and handed it to Noah. "Your favorite, I think."

Noah dropped the candy bar into the pocket of his shirt. "I meant . . . You haven't dated anyone? Don't you want to . . . eventually get married? Maybe if he knows you're seeing someone, he'll leave you alone."

Aaron had left her alone. Crying on the kitchen floor. Because he wanted to see other people.

*If only he'd meant it.*

"This morning, I asked my Magic Eight Ball if he'd ever stop calling."

Noah chuckled. "I thought you were going to throw that out. What'd it say?"

"Prospects are brightening. I thought maybe I'd meet someone here, but I know everyone."

Noah's blue eyes locked on hers. He seemed to be searching for something. "Do you have to meet someone new?"

Daphne started to say, "Well, of course," but stopped. *Did she? What if she had already met the man of her dreams? What if he'd been waiting his turn in line and she hadn't talked to him. Just handed him a candy bar and turned to the next guest. What if she'd known him forever and never thought of him that way?* She surveyed the guests, searching out the single men she knew. That crowd was getting thinner.

There was Ray, but he liked to play the field, with a different woman every week. And Noah, but he couldn't be the man of her dreams. They'd been friends for far too long. A spark would have flared earlier. Not exploded five minutes ago.

Although, if she hadn't known him her whole life, she'd be ogling him like any other red-blooded female. Those muscled arms, his caring smile, and that cologne. *That cologne. That must be the difference. He probably splashed extra on to cover the smoke smell.*

The chime rang again. "I don't want to miss a chance to apologize to Miranda where she can't beat me to a pulp." He touched her shoulder and ventured onto the dance floor. Daphne hugged herself, feeling strangely bereft without him by her side.

He planted a kiss on Miranda's cheek and gave her a congratulatory hug. Miranda playfully punched him in the arm, but smiled brightly at him as they danced. She must have forgiven him quickly. But then, today had been Miranda's dream, every detail perfect, from the sunny weather to the blooming rhododendrons around the garden pavilion.

Daphne forced a smile for the next man in line and exchanged his dollar for a candy bar. She gave him a quick once-over. Decent haircut. Nice shoes. A possibility. He was one of the groom's relatives, so she explained her connection to Miranda and deftly stepped aside when he tried to grope her behind. Perhaps that was the purpose of the dreaded butt-bow: to protect unsuspecting bridesmaids from being fondled by inebriated guests. Thankfully, the chime rang before he could attempt another feel, and he was off to slobber a kiss on Miranda.

After his dance, Noah started across the floor toward her, but a group of mutual friends waved him over to the bar. The Dollar Dance finally ended. Daphne retreated from her post and deposited her basket with the Mistress of Ceremonies, snagging the last Hershey's Special Dark for herself.

Noah waved her over. "Want to dance?"

"Sure." She followed him to the dance floor. He pulled her into his arms and they swayed to the music. She expected the casual comfort she usually felt when Noah touched her. She didn't get it. Her nerves sparked like downed power lines. Miranda and Max playfully bumped into them as they spun around the floor. Miranda grinned at Max like he was her prince. They kissed.

"It's the romantically tinged atmosphere of the wedding," she muttered, as Noah twirled her around and they proceeded to bump Beth and Jake.

"What was that?" Noah asked.

"You know, I've danced at weddings in every color. Purple, blue, yellow, Barbie pink, several times." She nodded toward her dress. "But never white."

"It's not a bad thing it didn't work out with Aaron."

"I know. It's better to know he's a weasel now rather than to be stood up at the altar, but it doesn't make it hurt any less. At least he could have had the guts to break up with me in person. Maybe then I wouldn't be taken in every time he calls. Sorry, I shouldn't say things like that about your cousin." She sighed. "But whenever he calls . . ."

"It reminds you of it all over again," Noah finished for her. "You're the only one he calls anymore. I think he's really messed up."

"He sounds so contrite about cheating on me. About how much he regrets it. I've stopped falling for it and I shouldn't dwell on it." She shook her head. "What about you? Do you think you'll ever get married?"

Noah looked away. She saw resentment and disappointment cross his face. "I want to. But it's complicated."

Daphne wanted to ask why, but the tight look on his face told her he didn't want to talk about it. The first beats of the "Hokey Pokey" blared from the speakers. Noah hurriedly steered her off the floor and toward the bar. "Do you have any practical jokes planned for Miranda's apartment while they're on their honeymoon?"

"I have a couple of things, but I have to go tomorrow morning. The rest of the week is busy with Beth's wedding. You want to come? I could really use your truck." Her heart skipped a beat, anticipating his answer. She only needed his truck. Anyone's large vehicle would do.

"You aren't going to fill my truck bed with water again, are you?"

"Hey, a rolling pool would have been a good idea if your truck hadn't been so rusty. It was still fun, even if we only made it a block before all the water spilled out. I do need help hauling stuff, though. Then I won't have to make four trips with my car." *And it will be a good way to prove she and Noah are only friends and this fleeting spark is only the magic of the wedding.*

## Chapter Two

Miranda's youngest sister, Jamie, dashed across the pavilion. She grabbed Daphne's arm and jerked her away from Noah. Daphne stumbled after her.

"We forgot to decorate their car!" Jamie exclaimed in a stage whisper, her eyes shiny with too much excitement. Daphne wondered if the high school student had been sucking the helium out of the balloon decorations.

"The groomsmen are in charge," Daphne said, trying to disengage her arm from Jamie's clenched fingers.

Jamie rolled her eyes. "All they brought was a pack of water balloons that look like grenades and paint-ball pellets. What did they think they were going to do with those? What do those have to do with weddings?"

"That's probably all they had in their trunk." Daphne scanned the tables, trying to remember where she'd stowed her poorly-dyed-to-match orange shoes. She found them and shoved her feet into the ugly sandals, then followed Jamie to the car.

The groomsmen seemed more excited about their plastic cups of beer than about decorating the car.

"Look. There's plenty of balloons and string around here. We can get some pop cans and tie them to the bumper. It'll be fine," she reassured the wailing maid of honor.

The groomsmen returned and they set to work tying bouquets of balloons to the side mirrors and bumpers. One of the groomsmen used a Swiss army knife to poke holes in the pop cans. Daphne sat on the curb and wove string through the holes of the cans. While she was tying one of the knots, the can slipped and she cut her thumb on the jagged hole.

Jamie scurried over when Daphne hissed in pain. The wound quickly bubbled with blood and Daphne instinctively stuck her thumb in her mouth to keep it from dripping.

"Oh my gosh! You're bleeding!" Jamie gasped. Daphne made a mental note to recruit her for the fall play at the high school. Anyone hearing her would think Daphne had sliced off her whole hand.

"I'll get Noah. He knows first aid." She hurried off with Daphne calling after her, "It's barely a scratch."

The cut hadn't stopped bleeding when Jamie returned with Noah in tow. Daphne shook her head at the medical kit Noah clutched. "I don't think all that's necessary. I just nicked it on a pop can. It'll stop bleeding in a minute."

Noah set the case down on the ground beside where she crouched. He knelt next to her and flipped the lid open.

*The sandalwood cologne again.* It drifted intoxicatingly over her.

After searching for a moment, he found a package of antiseptic and a bandage.

"Let's have a look." He reached for Daphne's hand. "If it doesn't need a bandage, I could kiss it and make it better." He winked.

"Ha ha," she said, but her pulse jumped at the thought. She reluctantly held out her wound to him. "It's really not bad." Blood welled from the small gash and threatened to drip down the side of her hand.

Noah placed a piece of gauze on the cut. He held her hand

carefully in his, applying pressure. With his other hand, he tore open the package of antiseptic.

"This may sting." He removed the gauze and oozed the antiseptic over her thumb.

Daphne gasped.

Noah glanced up at her. "You okay?"

Her ability to breathe vanished.

It was as if she'd never seen his eyes before. Blue like Caribbean water. Little gray flecks circled the irises and she wondered why she'd never noticed them. When she finally managed to nod, Noah skillfully wrapped the bandage around her wound.

"All set, but just in case . . ." He pressed his lips gently to the bandaged thumb. She felt his warm breath against her open palm. Her pulse pounded so hard, she could almost see it throb in her wrist.

"Do you kiss all the cuts you bandage?" she asked, striving for a joking tone. He'd probably bandaged hundreds of them at traffic accidents he'd been to with the fire department.

"Only if they're on bridesmaids." He released her hand and she allowed it to fall back into her lap.

"Thanks. You didn't have to go through all this trouble."

"No problem. You wouldn't have wanted blood on your dress." He smiled and brushed the taffeta flare of her skirt. His fingertips grazed the bare skin on the back of her calf.

Daphne felt her face flush. *What was going on? Was he flirting with her? He never flirted with anyone. Did he feel sorry for her?*

"It's not like I'm going to wear it again. Unless you want me to."

Noah laughed and closed his kit.

*Or was she flirting with him?*

The groomsmen pronounced the Mustang done. Twenty cans

trailed behind the car and someone had even scrawled "Just Maried" on a soda can carton and tacked it to the rear bumper.

The English teacher in her barely registered the missing *r.* Her thoughts were still clouded by the clear blue of Noah's eyes.

## Chapter Three

Daphne wrangled the plastic covering over her bridesmaid dress and stuffed it in the closet. She should probably dry clean it before storing it, but the next time this dress saw the light of day, it would be on its way to Goodwill. Her friends always said they wanted to pick flattering dresses, but she'd ended up with Drag Queen Barbie's wardrobe.

The doorbell rang as she slid the bi-fold door closed.

Who would be coming over at this hour? She glanced down at the tank top and shorts she'd pulled on to make sure they were decent. Not flattering, but any visitor at midnight shouldn't be expecting her to open the door, let alone be dressed for a garden party. She peered through the peephole and blinked. Looked again and stepped back.

Blue eyes.

Noah?

Giddiness rushed over her. Like she was in high school and saw her first crush. She took a calming breath, but her senses tingled as she opened the door.

"Hey, Noah . . ." She trailed off.

She'd never gotten them confused before.

Aaron leaned against the door jamb with one arm above his head. His clothes were rumpled and he smelled like a rotting sandwich dipped in beer.

"You look like hell," she said, her eyes stinging. "Smell like it, too."

Aaron pushed himself off the door jamb and squinted at the light pouring out of her door.

"Well, no one would believe you were the Homecoming Queen," he snapped. "You've really let yourself go."

"What are you doing here?" she asked, wondering why she hadn't slammed the door in his face. Her hand gripped the door knob. Something about him seemed off, and he didn't look like he should be driving.

"Huh. Yeaaah." He laughed. "What time is it anyway? Were you waiting for me?" He shaded his eyes. "Could you turn down the lights? I have a nasty headache."

"Have you been drinking?" Daphne leaned against the door and rubbed her forehead. She didn't have the energy to play his games tonight.

"Not a thing, babe." He shook his head, grimacing in pain.

"Not a thing that you remember," Daphne muttered. He swayed toward her and she got a blast of his breath. He smelled like he'd gargled with cheap beer three weeks ago and hadn't brushed his teeth since.

Aaron laughed again.

She stepped behind the door to ward off the foul wave of his breath.

"Go home, Aaron. Back to your hotel room, or your mom's, or whatever ditch you crawled out of." Daphne edged the door closed.

Aaron shoved his hand through the opening and grabbed the door.

"Can I stay here?"

Daphne didn't even think about that one. "Heck, no."

"Just for tonight. I don't have a hotel room and I can't let my mom see me like this."

If he went home to Mama, Daphne'd hear all about how

Aaron was never the same after she dumped him. How could she have been so cruel? It was the same story every time Aaron came home just a little more down on his luck.

"What about all your friends?" She thumped her palm against her forehead. "That's right. You crapped all over them, just like you did to me."

"Daphne, please." His voice was suddenly more sober. "Just tonight and then I'll be gone. I won't hang around."

"No. You can park your car at the Walmart and sleep there. I don't care." Daphne shook her head.

"I think I did that today."

"You think? You don't remember?"

He laughed again. "Nope. Funny how that happens. Pretty frequently too. Can I at least take a shower?"

Because she suspected his foul odor would embed itself into her entryway if he stood there much longer, she relented.

"One shower and you sleep on the couch, but you're out of here by six."

"Okay." He tried to push through the doorway, but Daphne blocked his path. If she was going to put up with him for the next six hours, she was going to get something out of it.

"And I never hear from you again."

"Whatever."

"I don't do 'whatever' on this one. I need a promise." She jabbed her finger into his chest. She wanted to put Aaron behind her and move on. She couldn't do that when he called her once a month. How would she do it if he showed up on her doorstep whenever he was too hungover to go home? She should have stopped answering his calls after the one where he dumped her.

"I promise," he hissed. "Do you want to pinky swear, too?" He held up his hand and crooked his little finger.

Daphne scowled at him and motioned him through the door. She'd dip her finger in acid before she'd touch Aaron again.

He breezed past her as smoothly as if he'd had nothing but lemonade all day. She narrowed her eyes at his back. *Was the whole hangover an act?* She wouldn't put it past him, but her conscience wouldn't let him drive if it wasn't. He wandered into the living room, obviously ready to make himself at home.

Every cell in her body screamed this was a bad idea, but it was also a reminder of all the bad things about him. Things she needed to remember the next time he called. She had no doubt he would, all promises aside. She took another sniff of the foul haze around him and gagged. *Just remember that,* she warned herself.

Her resolve from yesterday had barely lasted twenty-four hours. *What would Noah think if he saw her now? Letting Aaron stay overnight. She would be stronger next time.*

She directed him to the bathroom and gave him a clean towel from the linen closet. She retrieved an extra set of sheets and spread them over the couch, secretly glad the springs were busting out of their forms. Hopefully, it'd make him think twice about trying to camp out at her place again.

A few moments later, Aaron emerged from the bathroom wrapped in his towel. The football helmet tattoo on his left pectoral sagged without the bulging muscle underneath it. It drooped over his empty six-pack abs. The towel threatened retreat as Aaron sauntered into the living room.

"What are you doing?" Daphne screeched, slapping her hand over her eyes. "Where are your clothes?"

"They smelled really bad. I couldn't put them back on after taking a shower."

Daphne wondered how long he'd been wearing them. His whole outfit looked like it'd been slept in. *Had he really slept in his car all day?* "Don't you have clean ones in the car?"

"No. I was planning to go home Friday night." He shook his head. "That's really weird. I have this huge blank spot in my memory. What day is it?"

"Saturday. Early Sunday, actually. I'll see if I can find something that will fit." Daphne went to her office and dug through the garbage bags of clothes she'd set aside for Goodwill. She found a pair of extra-large pink sweatpants she'd used for a skit at school. They were the only thing that would remotely fit him. The "powder puff" across the backside made her smile. Subtle revenge. He'd never get it.

She threw the pants at him.

"Sweatpants? It's eighty degrees in here."

"You're not going commando and it's all I've got."

He started to drop the towel.

"In the bathroom." She pointed. He'd never grown out of his high school obnoxiousness. It made her wonder what she saw in him then.

Aaron tossed the pants over his shoulder and went into the bathroom to change. She showed him the couch, then headed for the bathroom herself to get ready for bed.

He'd taken his clothes off as if they were infested with bees, flinging them all around the room. She gathered them up, feeling sorry for his mother, and threw them in the washing machine. She stuck his shoes on the back steps to let them air out. Besides alcohol and sweat, there was a familiar scent on his clothes she couldn't place.

When she returned to the living room, he had stretched out on the couch with his arms folded behind his head. Satisfied he was wearing the sweatpants, she headed for her bedroom.

"I'm going to bed. Remember, out by six."

"What's the hurry? You got a date or something?" he called.

"Or something," she mumbled. She couldn't let Noah see Aaron here when he picked her up in the morning. He'd never believe how she could let Aaron worm his way in here. She couldn't believe it herself. But Aaron seemed like he was in trouble. Or troubled. Or both.

Maybe a semi-decent night's sleep and he'd be back to his

old self. He would have to get it somewhere else, though, because there was no sleeping comfortably on that couch.

Daphne closed the door to her bedroom, wishing she could lock it. Noah had freaked her out with stories about people being trapped in a fire because of a locked bedroom door, so she'd had the handle changed. Okay, he'd only told her one story, but she didn't want to be the second. She grabbed her book off the nightstand and had barely read three pages when there was a knock on the door.

She scowled. "What?"

"I can't sleep. I saw your light on. Could we talk?" Aaron's voice was rough, as if he'd just woken up. He couldn't have slept in the ten minutes since she'd gone to bed.

"About what?" She couldn't think of a single thing she wanted to talk to him about. She'd told him everything she'd had to say on the phone when he'd called on Friday.

"Us."

*That wouldn't even make the list.*

"The only thing I'd want to talk about is how quickly you'll be leaving in the morning."

She heard his hand touch the doorknob.

"Don't even think about opening the door." Her voice cracked as she spoke. She pulled her quilt up to her chest. She was still wearing the tank top and shorts, but it felt more risqué in bed. She couldn't let him in here.

"Daphne, are you sure you don't want to get back together?"

"Yes!" She resisted the urge to throw her book at the door. She liked Jane Austen too much to abuse her that way. It was too bad she'd finished *War and Peace* last week. That would've put a hole in her door.

"But why?"

"You sound like a six-year-old."

"Can't we talk face to face? Clear things up?" The doorknob rattled again.

She reached for the phone on her nightstand. She moved her thumb between the emergency preset and Noah's. Noah'd find out either way. All emergency calls requiring response went to the fire department pagers, even if they weren't required to respond.

"Touch that knob again and I'm calling for help."

She heard a thud and a creak and guessed he had leaned against the linen closet door.

"You dumped me with that horrible phone call, remember? You made it quite clear I was no longer good enough for you by dating other people. I don't understand why you keep calling me."

"I was wrong. I miss you so much. I thought we were good together." His voice took on a whiny tone, making her cringe. "I made a mistake. Can't you forgive me?"

"Forgiving you doesn't require dating you."

"We could be friends for a while first. . . . It'd be like old times."

"Friends shouldn't date. And forgiving you doesn't make you my friend either." She knew where this was leading. It was the same conversation they'd had on the phone. He wanted to relive his glory days in high school before he'd dumped all his friends for something bigger and better. The flashy Camaro, the glitzy job, and the attractive assistant with legs up to her armpits.

But life hadn't worked out all that well for Aaron. He tried to make it look like it did, but Daphne knew better. Sure, he had the clothes and the car, but something wasn't right. He didn't have his usual swagger.

Aaron hadn't said anything for a few minutes and Daphne thought he'd returned to the couch. She set the phone on her nightstand and opened her book. She'd just found her place when the doorknob rattled again.

"Do not come in here," she warned.

The door opened a couple of inches and Aaron poked his head through.

"The couch is lumpy."

"It's either the couch or the floor, but you are not sleeping in here."

"I promise I won't try anything." He put on his *Mom, can I please have a cookie?* look.

"I don't trust your promises." Daphne closed her book and shook her head. "Sorry, Jane," she muttered. She whipped the book at the door. It smacked against the wood so hard it rattled the door. The book thudded to the floor and Daphne winced as it landed facedown and open, the pages crinkled. She threw the quilt back.

"Okay. Okay." Aaron stepped through the doorway. He glanced back at her. "Aren't those my boxers?"

"No. Take your keys and get out of here."

"You're throwing me out?"

"I warned you about coming into my room." She shoved his shoulder and pushed him toward the door.

"You've got to be kidding." He tried to throw her hand away from him, but she kept pushing him. Straight to the door.

"What about my keys?" he called, as he stumbled down the steps.

Daphne grabbed them off the end table and hurled them down the stairs. They landed on the edge of the light cast by the open door.

Aaron scooped the keys off the gravel, mumbling something she didn't care to hear. She slammed the door shut, slid the chain in place, and twisted the deadbolt.

*He's never crossing my threshold again,* she thought.

## Chapter Four

W e can leave the Santas here. They're for the yard,"
Daphne directed, as Noah parked his truck in Max's driveway.
She pushed open the door of Noah's F-150. "Remember how
the doors of that old Ford Ranger used to creak? I expected
them to fall off every time I opened them." Daphne hopped
out and opened the rear door of the extended cab.

Noah withdrew the keys from the ignition and set them on
the center console. He looked over his shoulder at Daphne, who
was sorting through the grocery bags in the backseat. "Aaron
wanted me to weld them shut and jump in through the windows
like the Duke boys, until Dad reminded him the seats would get
soaked every time it rained."

Daphne stiffened while reaching into one of the bags.

Why had he brought Aaron up? He didn't need to remind
her of Aaron. Yesterday she'd said she was over him, but she
wouldn't react like this if she weren't still hurting.

*Nice,* Noah thought. *Way to rub salt in a skinned knee.*

He climbed out of the truck and heaved a box of flamingoes
out of the truck bed.

"Yeah. He liked flash. Bought that old Camaro and left you
with the Ranger," Daphne said, as she pulled a purple plastic
bag from the backseat.

"I wanted the Ranger. It was ugly, but it worked. The Camaro always had something wrong with it."

Daphne's features eased into a smile. "And you couldn't put a pool in the Camaro." Daphne grabbed a box of leprechaun figurines and the purple bag and bumped the rear truck door shut with her hip. She jogged up the house steps and deposited her boxes on the step next to the door. Her jogging shorts emphasized the muscles flexing in her toned legs as she climbed the stairs. He imagined caressing the smooth skin and almost dropped the box of faded pink flamingos he carried. She jiggled the square black mailbox attached to the house beside the door and caught the house key as it slipped free. After unlocking the door, she shoved her boxes inside and held the door open for him.

Glancing in the box as he passed, she said, "Those go in the bathroom."

"Gotcha." He headed down the hallway.

"What's the plan for these?" He placed the box on the closed toilet seat.

"We'll fill the tub with packing peanuts and float the flamingoes on top. I've got a bunch of treasures to hide in there too." Daphne pulled a pack of cards out of the grocery bag. "I found these at the adult book store, but I wanted to attach them to the leprechauns and hide them around the house. These can go in the tub." She extracted six bottles of massage lotion and several colors of silky thong underwear. "And these can go on the flamingoes." She held up a silk blindfold and a feather boa.

Noah grabbed the blindfold and twirled it in his fingers. "This may be more than I want to know about Max and Miranda."

"Don't think about it that way," Daphne scolded. "It won't be any fun." She snatched the blindfold away and tossed it back in the bag. "I'll get the packing peanuts."

Noah picked up the pack of cards and dumped them into his hand. He flipped through them and felt his ears grow warm. Where had Daphne found these?

Noah had loved Daphne since second grade, when she dropped a Twinkie on the ground. He'd snatched it out of the dirt well within the time limit and offered it to her. Daphne had refused to eat it even after he'd explained the ten-second rule about germs.

Her refusal didn't stop her from kicking him in the shin when he stuffed the whole thing in his mouth. The creamy center oozed through the gap where his front teeth should have been, and that earned him another kick. She'd insisted he trade one of the homemade chocolate chip cookies from his lunch box for the Twinkie he stole. He'd refused until she nailed him in the shin again and took the cookie anyway. They'd been friends ever since, and his heart had been lost.

Daphne returned with the packing peanuts and dumped them into the tub. "Have you thought of anything for us to bet on for Beth and Jake's wedding yet?"

Noah glanced down at the card in his hand. It read, *Kiss passionately in a public place.* "How 'bout this?" He showed Daphne the card.

"During the ceremony? Beth would never. She's very particular about public displays of affection. I think their kiss will be very quick."

"Not if Jake has anything to say about it."

Daphne shook her head. "Beth's been very adamant. She hates it when people are all over each other. She wanted to yell 'Break it up!' at Miranda's wedding."

"I think we have our bet." He held out his hand and Daphne shook it.

He shoved the cards back in the box and dropped it in the grocery bag. Daphne shoved the lotions into the peanuts and placed the flamingoes on top. She tied the blindfold on one and wrapped the feather boa around another.

"What's next?" Noah asked.

"The leprechauns and the cards. I've got a paper punch and some ribbon. We can tie the cards to the figurines and then hide them around the house. They'll be finding these for months." She giggled.

Noah couldn't help but laugh too. He loved how she got excited about little things. "Is there any significance to the leprechauns, or don't I want to know?"

"No. I found them at Goodwill for cheap and they're kind of creepy." She held one up. "They look like they have a dirty secret, don't you think?"

"Well, they will when you attach the cards."

They sat down at the kitchen table to attach the cards and figurines. Noah punched holes and Daphne tied ribbons.

"So yesterday," Daphne said, "you said getting married would be complicated. Why's that?"

Noah punched a couple of cards before answering.

"It just is."

Daphne dropped the card and ribbon on the table. "It just is? What kind of answer is that? It just is. Haven't we been friends forever?"

"Yeah." He reached for another card.

"How is it complicated?"

*How do you explain you're in love with your cousin's girl-friend? Well, ex-girlfriend. You watched him hurt her so badly you didn't think she'd ever recover. You wanted to make it right, but you didn't know how. And even then you wouldn't be worthy of her.*

He couldn't tell her that.

The solution would have to be complicated, but if he could find a way to straighten everything out . . . then he might have a chance. He and Daphne worked so well together, especially with practical jokes. She had the inspiration, he had the know-how. She had the bikini and wanted a hot tub; he had the rusty truck. His thoughts derailed at the memory of that little white string bikini against her tanned skin. He remembered quite distinctly that it didn't look like she had any tan lines.

"I have to figure out how to fix something first." He stopped, searching for words. *Could he just tell her he loved her? That he would rather love her from afar than date someone else?*

"Like what?" Daphne set a beribboned leprechaun on the table and reached for another.

"It's complicated." If he could find a way to make up for what Aaron did to her, then maybe he would let himself think about it. Aaron had almost destroyed her. After two years, Noah was finally seeing the old Daphne return.

"You said that. How?" She twisted a green ribbon around her finger.

"Can I take a rain check on that?"

"No. Come on, Noah. What is it? You usually tell me everything." She grasped his hand.

Her touch burned.

*Except one thing,* he thought, sliding his hand away.

Daphne looked down at his hand and then up at his face. "This is serious, isn't it?" She leaned forward. Her gaze held his and he couldn't look anywhere else.

Noah eased back in his chair and rubbed his hand over his newly trimmed hair. He needed to put some space between them before he made a bigger mess of things. He looked down at the deck of cards in his hand. That didn't help. He turned the deck over.

"Can I help you figure it out?" Daphne asked.

Noah sighed. "I need time to sort it all out."

Daphne pursed her lips, but seemed to get the hint. "What about one detail? I have to say I'm intrigued. I've never seen you date anyone more than once or twice."

Noah blew out a deep breath. "Daphne, if I give you one hint, you'll figure it all out. Because it involves other people, I can't talk about it until I can fix it."

Daphne's eyes narrowed, then she relaxed in her chair. "Fair enough, but if I can help you, let me know. You've been there for me and I'll be here for you."

Noah punched the last card and flipped it at Daphne.

She picked up the card and read the instructions on it. She arched her eyebrow at him. "Would this work?"

"If it was as easy as champagne and chocolate, I'd have six children." Noah scooped up a few of the figurines. "Where do you want these?"

"Any little nook and cranny will do. Preferably not right out in the open." Daphne grabbed one and hid it behind Max's bowling trophy. She continued to place them around the living room, peering out from behind a stack of books or in the drawer of the coffee table.

Noah looked helplessly at the leprechauns in his hands. Every time he thought of a spot, Daphne had already hidden one there.

"You haven't hid any yet." Daphne grabbed a leprechaun out of his hand and pulled him into the kitchen. She tried to slide one on the highest shelf by the sink. As she reached up, her T-shirt came untucked and Noah saw the graceful curve of her waist. He forgot the figurines in his hands. The figures slid out of his grip and smashed onto the floor. He barely registered the sound. He grasped her waist and lifted her up, and she tucked the leprechaun behind the leaves of the plant. Electricity burned through his hands and up his arms, almost knocking him off balance. Her body slid through his hands as he lowered her to the ground, his fingers brushing tantalizingly across her skin. He withdrew reluctantly, dropping his hands to his sides.

Daphne stepped away from him and tucked her T-shirt back in. She looked down at the leprechauns scattered on the linoleum. The head had snapped off one and another had lost an arm. Daphne knelt and snatched the broken pieces. She moved to toss them in the trash, but Noah stopped her.

"We can still use them."

"A headless leprechaun? That's too creepy," Daphne said, moving toward the garbage can.

"I've got some super glue in the truck. I can have them back to themselves in no time."

Daphne pondered the dismembered figures in her hands and then the worn linoleum. "They're not worth it. We've got plenty spread around. They'll just have to do."

"What about these cards?" Noah picked up the freed cards from the floor. "They're good ones." He flipped one over and raised his eyebrows. "Really good ones."

Daphne snatched the cards from his hands and started to crumple them. "Toss them with the leprechauns, I guess."

"Let me see if I can glue them back together first. It'd be a shame to waste, what? How much did you spend on these?"

"Twenty-five cents."

"Each?"

"Total. Just chuck them."

"I'll fix them while you hide the rest."

She seemed to hesitate, then put the broken pieces in his hand. She scooped the intact figures off the countertop. "I'll hide these in the bedrooms and the office. Then we can start unloading the Santas." She stepped around him and hurried down the hallway. About halfway down, she stopped and turned. "You know, Noah, you don't have to fix everything. Some things are broken beyond repair."

## Chapter Five

Daphne dropped the last leprechaun in the laundry hamper and flipped the lid closed. She stepped back and rubbed her hand across her forehead. She'd stalled as long as she could, but her pulse still raced.

She went into the bathroom and turned on the cold tap. She held her wrist under the cool stream of water. Pressing her damp wrist to her forehead, she tried to get control of herself.

Ever since Noah lifted her, it had set her off balance. Well, actually since she'd smelled his aftershave at Miranda's wedding. *What was going on?* Why had she suddenly noticed Noah's cologne and his eyes? Why was she hyperaware of him? The way he moved. The tone of his voice. She was sensitive to his every breath.

It was almost the same feeling she'd had when she first saw Aaron. The heady giddiness. The quaking in her stomach and legs. The warm shivers blushing through her body.

She had to put a stop to this. She couldn't be attracted to Noah. She'd known him forever. Nothing had changed between them. He was still her good friend and that was all she wanted him to be. Really, she told herself, that was all she wanted. Anything else would jeopardize their friendship.

Noah had shown up the night Aaron dumped her. She'd been sitting on the floor in the kitchen, the phone on the floor

beside her and the potato salad she'd made for his family reunion rotting on the counter. Noah sat on the floor next to her.
He didn't say a word.

He nudged a box of tissues toward her, but she didn't need
it. The tears wouldn't come.

She did devour the quart of Mackinac Island Fudge ice
cream he'd brought. Her favorite flavor. She thought he might
have taken a bite or two, but she couldn't remember. She woke
up in her bed with the tissues beside her, not recalling how she
got there. The last thing she remembered was leaning against
Noah's shoulder and the tears finally running down her cheeks.

Which made her reaction to him today all the more weird.
She turned off the faucet and dried her wrist and her face on
the hand towel. Glancing out the window, she glimpsed Noah.

People always commented on it, but she'd never mixed Noah
and Aaron up until last night. Physically, sure, their frames and
colorings were similar. But their personalities were nothing
alike. Aaron, she had come to realize, only wanted things and
people for how they reflected on him. The sports car, the homecoming queen. Noah drove a rusty truck so he could save for
college. He volunteered for the fire department.

Maybe she was just attracted to the physical resemblance
between Noah and Aaron. Her mind was pretending Noah was
Aaron because she missed the good times with Aaron.

But she'd felt nothing but loathing when Aaron showed up
last night. *What would Noah think if he knew Aaron had been
there? That she'd agreed to let him sleep on her couch?* After
telling Noah she wouldn't let Aaron get to her anymore, she'd
let him into her house. Maybe she wasn't as strong as she
thought. Best just to stay away from both of them.

*Ignore these emotions,* she scolded herself in the mirror. Taking a fortifying breath, she headed for the front yard and found
Noah standing among the Santas like a giant among elves. He
scratched the back of his head as he looked down at the

knee-high plastic figures. His muscled frame looked large and comforting against the elfin backdrop.

Her heart fluttered.

*Damn.*

She pushed it aside. *Calm,* she told herself. Focus on the lawn ornaments and everything will return to normal.

"What do you want to do with these?" He picked up one of the Santas and balanced it on his hand. It wobbled side to side and he moved his hand to steady it.

Her gaze traveled up his arm to the muscles flexing there. Her mouth went dry.

*Double damn.*

This was so not happening. This was Noah. Not Aaron. Not George Clooney. Not Brad Pitt. Not even Hugh Jackman. Well, maybe Hugh Jackman.

Daphne cleared her throat. "I painted glow-in-the-dark letters on their bellies. It dries almost clear." She walked over to the crowd and picked one up. She tilted it side to side, trying to catch the light reflecting on the paint. "This one has an *N* on it."

Noah examined the one he had been balancing. "I think this one has an *O*."

Daphne glanced at it. "Yep. I didn't realize the paint would be so hard to see when it dried."

"What does it spell?"

" 'Naughty or nice?' I wanted to line them up along the driveway so Max and Miranda would see them as soon as they got home. They're supposed to get in late, so they should see the message."

"I don't even want to know where you got that idea." Noah placed his Santa on the ground and picked up another one.

"A girl's got to have some secrets," she said, then clamped her mouth shut. *What was that? Flirting?* She definitely needed to work harder at this suppressing thing.

Noah grabbed another Santa and tilted it around. "Hey, Vanna, I got an *N*."

Daphne examined another Santa and tossed it to him. "There's two *N*s. Would you like to spin the wheel again?"

Noah placed the plastic figures in their proper places. "No, I'd like to buy a *Y*."

Daphne rolled her eyes and she rearranged the G and the H. "You can't buy a *Y*. It's not a vowel."

"Now here's where the English teacher's wrong." He crossed his arms over his chest. "Vowels are *A, E, I, O,* and *U,* and sometimes *W* and sometimes *Y*. In this case, *Y* is a vowel. It sounds like E."

Daphne held up her hand. "That's not how the game works. Why buy something you could get for free?"

"Maybe I think it's worth it." A mischievous grin accentuated his dimples.

Daphne suppressed a laugh. She shoved the *Y* Santa under her arm and waited, tapping Santa's head with her fingertips. *Keep the mood light,* she thought. *It'll keep my mind on the task at hand.* "I don't think you have two hundred and fifty dollars. Or do they cost more now? I haven't watched *Wheel of Fortune* in so long."

"Maybe I have something better." He wiggled his eyebrows suggestively.

She stopped tapping her fingers as her mind flew through all the things something better might be. "And what might that be?" she finally asked.

He scratched his head, then burst out laughing. Shaking his head, he said, "A super-glued leprechaun."

Daphne couldn't help but smile. "You bozo." She tossed the Santa to him. He caught it easily and placed it in the line-up. Daphne plunked the *E* Santa between the *C* and the question mark and stepped to the end of the driveway to survey their work.

She loved the easy banter she had with Noah. Their relationship was just right the way it was. She wasn't going to let anything change it.

Even if she did find him breathtakingly attractive.

## Chapter Six

Noah clicked his e-mail closed. No ranting message from Coach Reynolds. Better than he expected for this Monday morning.

He glanced out the window and his mind retreated to its usual topic: Daphne and how to make up for what Aaron did to her. He doodled Daphne's name on his notepad and then tapped his pen against the desk. He knew he couldn't erase how Aaron had dumped her, but maybe he could help her put Aaron firmly in the past. He didn't think that would open the way for him, but if Daphne was happy that was a start.

According to his calendar, he had Friday night open. Maybe he could take Daphne to that restaurant down on the lake. He knew she'd never been there with Aaron, so it wouldn't have any terrible associations.

He picked up his office phone and dialed her number, waiting through a series of rings until her answering machine picked up. Her voice on the machine reminded him of the kiss he'd brushed across her hand.

*The first time he'd allowed his lips to touch her skin.*

He forgot his prepared speech. Her machine beeped.

"Hi, uh Daphne. Noah, here." He laughed nervously. "I wanted to talk about Friday. I mean, see if . . . I mean this coming Friday. Not last Friday. Ha ha. It's just that I was wondering what's going on with you . . ." *Crap*. He stopped talking. This wasn't coming out right. He sounded like he was drunk-dialing.

He was about to give up and say he would call back when he heard Daphne pant, "Hello?"

"Hi, Daphne, it's Noah."

"Sorry. I missed the phone. I was outside."

Noah pictured her lounging on her deck with an umbrella drink and one of those massive old books she liked. Well, maybe not the umbrella drink. It was only ten in the morning.

"No problem. Are you busy Friday night? There's this great place on the lake I thought you might like."

He pictured her glancing at the calendar on the wall above the phone, tracing her finger to the date he suggested.

"That sounds like fun."

Noah's heart leapt, but she continued speaking.

"Unfortunately, I'm in Beth's wedding on Saturday and the rehearsal is Friday evening. I'm sorry."

Noah scrolled through his own calendar and saw the notation there for Beth's wedding on Saturday. He wasn't part of the wedding party and wouldn't be going to the rehearsal. It should have occurred to him that since Beth and Daphne were best friends, Daphne's whole weekend was probably packed with wedding stuff. He'd be lucky to snag a dance at the reception.

"Of course. Maybe some other time, then?" he asked, not wanting to push too hard right away.

"I'll let you know. With all these weddings this summer, my weekends are all pretty busy."

Noah hung up the phone, saying he'd see her at the wedding. It felt like he had just been shot down, but he knew she wasn't lying. She did have a lot of weddings. All their single friends had paired up and they were the only two left.

He scribbled in the bubbles of the letters on his blotter, mulling over the conversation. *Was she turning him down com-*

*pletely? Did she know he was asking her on a date, not just a hang out thing?* She had to know he was interested in pursuing something more with her. He'd tried to hint at his interest before, but wanted to keep his distance until she seemed ready. She seemed really relaxed at Miranda's wedding, but maybe that had been the champagne. Her weekends were really busy, but there had to be another time.

His phone rang.

He picked up the oversized handset and slid over his Carterville Hornets notepad.

"I know this is last minute, but I can't coordinate the Power Up Girls program this summer," Phyllis said. Phyllis was the physical education teacher for the elementary school, and he'd cajoled her into starting the program this year.

"Are you sure?" he asked. They already had several girls signed up and Noah really didn't want to drop the program.

"My dad had a stroke down in Florida. I'm going to be down there for the rest of the summer. I hate to drop this program, but I've got to be with my dad. There's no one else to take care of him."

"No. I understand." Noah scribbled "Power Up Girls" and "coordinator?" on his notepad. "Do you have anyone in mind for a replacement? An assistant who could take over for you?"

"I've been doing everything myself." Phyllis sighed. "I was hoping to entice a parent or two to help at the orientation. I can bring you my info this afternoon before I leave. Then at least you'll have it, if you find someone. Everyone I know who might be interested is already busy."

Noah hung up after wishing her father a speedy recovery. He reached for his Rolodex and dialed the other elementary physical education teachers, then the coaches of the other summer activities. All pleaded busyness with vacations and other summer programs. A couple just plain said no.

Carterville girls needed this program. It could reach a lot of vulnerable young girls not already involved in a team sport. He'd seen the statistics from other areas. Girls who participated in the program were more likely to do better in school, delay sexual activity, and avoid drug use. They also had fewer self-esteem issues.

Carterville was exactly why this program was designed. The number of teen pregnancies was growing each year, and the girls usually dropped out of high school, even junior high in one case. Carterville's female graduation rate was already below the state average, and Noah didn't want to see it drop any lower. High school was too late to connect with these girls. According to the research, catching the girls in late elementary and middle school while they still listened to adults made a huge difference.

Maybe he could lead it himself this year. At least for the first couple of meetings, and then he could get one of the parents to take over.

Phyllis had said the girls would meet three times a week and only run a mile for the first two weeks. Phyllis also mentioned some calisthenics and warm-up exercises. He could do that. Jumping jacks and stretches. Nothing he didn't do as part of his own workout routine.

He made some notes on his calendar, planning to coordinate the first meeting. Phyllis delivered the packet of information about the program. She had done all the legwork, for which Noah was thankful. She had the girls' schedule done and the parents' informational meeting agenda set. Her agenda and all the brochures were collated. Noah just had to read over the information and he'd be ready to go.

He paged through the file and found the agenda for the first meeting with the girls. Phyllis even included her welcome speech. He skimmed through it. It sounded like just the thing to pump up a group of third- through eighth-grade girls. His gaze screeched to a halt on the final words of the speech: "Let's dance."

*Dance?*

Phyllis had several songs listed, including "The Chicken Dance," "Girls Just Wanna Have Fun," and "Dancing Queen."

Noah shook his head. He couldn't do this. He didn't dance to fast songs. He especially didn't dance to girly songs. He leaned against the bar with his buddies as everyone else flailed around. He had to keep some self-respect. The girls definitely wouldn't be motivated to dance if they saw him doing it.

He was going to need help with this. But who else could he call? He'd tried everyone he knew.

Except the woman who was only busy on the weekends—the girls' high school cross-country coach. *Wouldn't she be perfect for this?*

He could help out with the non-dancing and the non-girly parts of the program. They'd get to spend more time together.

He picked up the phone and punched in Daphne's number. Her machine answered again, so he left an absolutely desperate, pleading message on her machine, hoping she would be able to help him out.

## Chapter Seven

Daphne untied her key from her running shoes and opened her apartment door. June was second only to October as her favorite time for running. The air was warm enough to easily work up a sweat, but cool enough that your clothes weren't soaked after a couple of miles. She'd put in five leisurely miles this morning, enjoying the breeze, the scenery, and stretching her muscles. She liked running alone during the summer. She could run at her own pace. During the school year, most of her runs were with the girls' cross-country team, so she had to adjust to their pace, either quicker with the fastest girls or almost walking with the girls who ran for exercise rather than competition.

She yanked her T-shirt over her head and wiped the glistening layer of sweat off her face and chest. Heading to the kitchen for a bottle of water, she noticed the answering machine blinking. She retrieved a water bottle from the refrigerator and glanced at the caller ID display.

Carterville High School—Athletic Director.

Noah again.

How was she supposed to avoid him if he called her all the time? This was the second time today. Was he asking her about the restaurant on the lake again? Beth's rehearsal dinner was the perfect excuse. And Noah couldn't object to it. Beth was her best friend.

What would she do if he asked her again? She wouldn't always have an excuse. Telling him she found him attractive was not an option. That would ruin their friendship and his ego for sure. After Aaron, her relationship radar was off. She couldn't trust it and she didn't want to lose a good friend because of it.

She'd see Noah every day at school in the fall. She had to get this attraction out of her system before then.

She snatched her Magic Eight Ball off the kitchen counter.

"Will I get him out of my system?" she asked, then shook the ball fiercely. She flipped it over and watched the cube float to the little window.

*I wouldn't count on it.*

Daphne snorted. She slammed the ball on the counter and headed for the shower. What did a stupid ball know anyway?

She chugged the last of her water and toed off her running shoes. Peeling off her socks, she turned on the faucet and wiggled out of the rest of her clothes as she waited for the hot water to travel up the pipes from the basement. As she tossed her clothes into the hamper, she realized she'd never listened to his message. She pushed the faucet closed, grabbed a towel, and hurried back to the phone.

When she punched the play button, Noah's voice responded.

"Daphne, it's Noah again. Sorry to bother you so much, but I've got a huge problem and I desperately hope you can help me. Phyllis has to go to Florida for a few weeks, and that leaves no one to run the Power Up Girls program. I've called everyone I can think of and you are my last hope. Please say you'll do it. I'll help in whatever way I can. I just can't run the meetings. It's important a woman do it and . . ." His voice got quiet. "I'll lose all my influence with Coach Reynolds if he hears I danced to 'Barbie Girl' in public. I'll owe you a huge favor if you can help me out with this. Call me."

Power Up Girls program? Where had she been when they were getting that started? She'd heard other coaches mention it and the great things it had done for their schools. She would have loved to be involved right from the beginning. She could certainly take over for Phyllis. She decided to call Noah after her shower since he'd left the office already anyway.

During her shower, she wondered how she'd missed the Power Up Girls stuff. It was exactly the type of program she would have championed. True, she'd been wrapped up in Aaron dumping her, but that had been over a year ago. Almost two, when she thought about it.

Two years. It was hard to believe it had been that long since he had unceremoniously kicked her to the curb. After telling her he had been sleeping with someone from his office for three months. His betrayal was like having her knee give out in the middle of a race. She hit the ground hard. She just stopped moving. She was still going through the motions of her life, teaching, coaching, and being a bridesmaid.

She watched everyone live their lives for two years, but she hadn't lived her own. Her friends were moving to the next stage. Getting married, having kids, filling their lives.

She stood on the sidelines, being a bridesmaid. *Why hadn't she moved on?* Found a new boyfriend, developed interests in more activities at school and in the community?

That required stepping out of the cushioned cocoon she'd wrapped herself in. Her friends knew her history, and they didn't push her to date or do new things. Of course, they were involved with planning their weddings and setting up their households.

And it wasn't that she hadn't dated anyone since Aaron. She had. They just weren't right for her.

She'd found something wrong with every eligible man put in front of her. Did it matter that Richard pronounced "Eyre" "ire" instead of "air"? Probably not. Or that Tim had spinach stuck in his teeth? No, again. She'd been looking for an excuse. The guy for her was out there, but she had to start looking. Beth's wedding would be the perfect place to start.

237

AID: A0000000043503
SEQ# 001351
AUTHORIZATION CODE - 350255
CHIP READ
TRANSACTION AMOUNT                         5.10
US DEBIT             VISA ************5314
CARD ISSUER              ACCOUNT#
MER# 258882

Change                                     0.00
Cashless                                   5.10

Take-Out Total                             5.10
Tax                                        0.10
Subtotal                                   5.00

2 L COKE                                    5.00

                                     Order 31
KS# 2              04/23/2018 04:10 PM

Power Up Girls would jumpstart her life, help her to see what was out there. She couldn't wait to tell Noah she wanted to do it.

The only problem was it meant seeing Noah a lot more than only at her friends' weddings. He said he would help with the meetings; he just didn't want to lead them. Even if she convinced him she didn't need his help, she'd be at school a lot more and probably run into him. How could she not? His office was across the hall from the gymnasium. She'd practically be tripping over him.

It was a risk she'd have to take. She could keep her attraction in control long enough to wave hello. She really wanted to lead this program.

Daphne turned off the water and grabbed her towel from the hook. She wiped off her face and wrapped the towel around her chest, tucking in the end. She hurried into the living room and grabbed the phone. She punched in Noah's office number and got his voice mail. She thumbed the off button and dialed his home number.

He answered with his usual "Yeah."

"You know that doesn't sound professional, don't you?" she said, sliding her toe through the puddle of water she was creating on the kitchen floor. She could have waited until she was dressed.

"I knew it was you. And I'm at home. Did you get my message?"

"Yeah. Why'd you wait so long to call me? You said I was your last hope."

"You haven't been up for volunteering for things lately. I didn't want to push you, but I ran out of people to call."

"That's flattering."

"I think you'd do a great job. I didn't think you'd be interested, that's all."

"Well, I am. What do you think about that?"

"Fantastic. Phyllis's got a lot done, so you won't have much prep work. I can drop off her stuff later this afternoon."

"Great. I'll be around."

"So what's it gonna be?"

"What?"

"The favor that you are going to extract from me. I'm your slave. Whatever you want."

An image flashed through her mind of him massaging her body. She could almost feel his hands traveling over her skin, relaxing and exciting at the same time. Her breathing tremored at the thought.

"Daphne? You there?"

"What?" She cleared her throat. She shook her head a little to clear the image. If she allowed images like that to invade her thoughts, she'd never be able to just wave to him in the hallway. She was supposed to be fighting them. "Oh. I'll think of something."

She hung up the phone and wandered over to her computer, intending to familiarize herself with the Power Up Girls mission before she got Phyllis' packet. She sat down, then realized she was still wrapped in her towel.

*Yeah, wave hello, whatever.* Noah was a distraction and she'd only talked to him on the phone. She was going to have to work extra hard to get over her attraction to him.

She went to her bedroom and pulled on a clean pair of underwear and shorts. She was digging through her drawer for a bra, when the doorbell rang.

That was fast, she thought, grabbing a sports bra and tugging it over her head. She wormed her way into a T-shirt and answered the door.

Her friend Beth stood on the other side with tears spilling down her cheeks, cradling a plastic bag filled with lime-green chiffon and satin.

"What am I going to do?" Beth wailed, pushing herself inside.

"What's wrong?" Daphne asked, closing the door behind her.

Beth tossed the mountain of fabric and plastic on Daphne's couch and flopped down next to it.

"I picked up the dresses from the boutique. They were two weeks late and I was getting frantic they wouldn't get here and my sister wouldn't have time to do the fittings. And now this." Beth dug through the tangle of fabric and withdrew a dress from the pile. "They're lime green!" she wailed. "I ordered sage! What am I going to do?"

"Maybe it's just the light," Daphne said, taking the dress and walking to the window. There was no mistaking the color. It was closer to the green reflective safety vests worn by construction workers than any shade of sage green. "What about the tuxedo vests? They're supposed to match the dresses, right?"

Beth nodded, sniffing. "They're sage. The exact color I wanted. We're going to look like a bunch of avocadoes."

"What did the boutique say about the mix-up?" Daphne examined the dress. The cut and the lines were beautiful and would have been flattering on her and Rachel. They just weren't the color Beth had chosen.

Daphne had been thrilled to have one bridesmaid dress that didn't look like she was auditioning for a makeover show. Unfortunately, that was no longer the case. The dresses were the color of vomit.

"They said there wasn't a mistake. This was the color I chose. I said this isn't sage green, but the lady just shrugged and said it must be their version of sage green because the color codes match." Beth buried her face in her hands. "This is awful. The guests will think you're there to direct traffic. I should have you carry stop signs and whistles."

Daphne draped the dress over a chair and wrapped her arms around Beth. "Good thing we're not wearing white gloves then, huh? You know we could carry those wands they use to direct planes at the airport. They would make fantastic bouquets.

We could do motions during the sermon." She waved her hands around as if she was preparing a plane to take off.

The corners of Beth's mouth turned up a little. She grabbed a pillow and swung it at Daphne. "Very funny."

"We could hand out peanuts and beverages from a cart as we go down the aisle. You'd have a whole theme."

"You've been spending too much time with Peggy."

"Oooh." Daphne winced. Her cousin Peggy would have added reflective tape to the tuxedoes and held the wedding at the airport. Thankfully, she hadn't planned anything that outrageous for her Fourth of July wedding. Yet. "You're right. Even she wouldn't go that far. I hope. We'll think of something for these dresses. We've got a few days. It only took us two hours to put together costumes for our stage rendition of *Wuthering Heights*. We can handle this." She tugged a tissue from the box and handed it to Beth.

Beth blotted her eyes, smearing mascara across her eyelids. Daphne picked up her dress and contemplated it. Every bride she knew went through hysterics over something. There should really be a psychology course for bridesmaids on temporary insanity.

She might have hysterics herself. She had to wear one of these neon monstrosities.

"Could we dye them?"

Beth shook her head. "I already called Rachel. She's on her way. She said the fabric won't take dye evenly, and then you'll look like you're wearing camouflage."

Daphne grimaced. Few brides wanted their bridesmaids to look like combat soldiers or deer hunters. Well, maybe Peggy would—if it went with her theme, of course. Good thing her wedding wasn't on Memorial Day or the opening day of deer hunting season.

"Did your sister have any other ideas?" Daphne asked, holding the dress up by the hanger and turning it from side to side.

The shoulder straps were narrow, but not so tiny you couldn't wear a bra, and the fitted bodice had a sweetheart neckline. The skirt had a little fullness to it, but that mostly came from the chiffon overlay.

"I didn't really ask," Beth said between sniffles. "I was so upset. I stopped here to have you try on your dress. Hopefully the sizes haven't been screwed up as well." She blew her nose loudly into the tissue and wadded it into a ball.

Daphne kept her thoughts about how well the ladies at the boutique took measurements to herself. All of her dresses had needed extensive alterations, and none of them in the same place. Beth didn't need to be reminded of that now.

"Do you want anything to drink?" Daphne draped the dress back on the pile and headed for the kitchen. "I've got some wine coolers."

"Sounds good. Heaven knows I could use a drink. What flavors?"

"Strawberry daiquiri. Wild raspberry and . . ." Daphne pushed the lemon lime back into the fridge. Beth probably wouldn't want a drink that reminded her of her disastrous bridesmaid dresses. "And cherry."

"Strawberry," Beth called from the couch.

Daphne selected cherry for herself and unscrewed the tops. She carried them around the counter separating her kitchen from her living room. She handed Beth her bottle and Beth tossed it back so quickly, she would have been gagging on the worm if it was tequila. Beth coughed and her eyes watered. She placed the bottle on a coaster and wiped her eyes with the back of her hand.

"It's not a shot. You can drink it in sips." Daphne smiled.

Beth nodded. "I just need it to work quickly. I'm so upset right now I can't even think."

"It's not a disaster. Who really cares what we lowly bridesmaids are wearing? Everyone will be focused on you, and you will look divine. Your dress fits perfectly and looks absolutely sweet on you." Daphne glanced over at her dress. "What do your flowers look like? Maybe the lime won't seem so Captain Safety with the flowers."

Beth heaved her purse off the floor and extracted her planner. Daphne had known it would be close by, because Beth had had it attached to her arm for the last nine months. Beth flipped a couple of pages and stopped on one with magazine photo cutouts of bouquets.

"The florist assured me they would look exactly like this." She pointed to a small cluster of white gardenias tied with a rose-colored ribbon. "What if she can't do that and I end up with clusters of dandelions? I heard of someone who paid a ton for flowers and ended up with swamp weeds around the altar." Beth fell back against the couch. "This is going to be a disaster. We should have eloped. Jake had the tickets to Vegas picked out." She burst into tears again.

Daphne patted Beth on the shoulder and sipped her own wine cooler. This could be a long afternoon.

Rachel arrived a few minutes later, sewing box in hand. She took one look at the dresses and gagged.

"I thought you were exaggerating. They look like radioactive snot. Why'd you pick such an ugly color?"

"I told you," Beth said between sniffs. "The color card was wrong. This is sage green." She shook the fabric in her fist.

Rachel rolled her eyes and plopped down on the ottoman. "Let's see if we have anything besides the color to worry about. Daphne, why don't you try your dress on? You may want your sunglasses, so you don't do permanent damage to your retinas. If we can't do something about the color, we'll have to hand them out at the wedding. Now there's an idea. Sunglasses would make good favors for the guests."

Daphne pulled the shades and peeled off her T-shirt and shorts, kicking them under the coffee table. She navigated her way through the filmy layers of chiffon and satin and arranged the dress to fit in the right places. She turned and held up her hair so Rachel could raise the zipper and do up the little hook at the top.

"I think it would fit fine without the sports bra," Beth said from her prone position on the sofa. "But with it the top gaps." She raised her drink, and Daphne was relieved to note the liquid hadn't descended much below the bottle label yet. Even in small amounts, alcohol made Beth sleepy.

"The sports bra's fine. It goes with the construction theme. We'll get you a hard hat and a traffic sign. Do you think you could get a shoe-leather tan and develop a smoker's cough before Saturday?" Rachel asked, as she twitched the skirt and studied the seams.

Daphne glanced down at the gray sports bra she'd pulled on after her shower when she had only planned on seeing Noah. "Very funny. Now you sound like Peggy. At least the dress fits everywhere else. That's a first. I'll go get my push-up bra and we'll see how it looks."

Daphne gathered up the skirt and tromped to her bedroom to retrieve the necessary bra. Bra in hand, she returned to the living room to find Beth and Rachel pouring over the pictures in Beth's planner. Rachel, upon seeing Daphne, jumped up to help her with the zipper of her dress. Daphne wiggled the bodice of the dress down and switched bras, working the cleavage shelf bra into place.

Rachel rezipped the dress and Daphne paraded around the sofa for Beth's opinion.

"Where'd you get those?" Beth giggled, pointing to the two mounds of flesh bursting above the neckline of the dress.

"They came with the bra." Daphne adjusted the neckline of the dress, tugging it this way and that, trying for something that wouldn't get her a job at Hooters. "I only filled the water reservoir to the second line."

Rachel studied the garment. "I can make adjustments here and here." She wove pins into the fabric to mark the places. "But I think we will need some double-sided tape to keep the girls in place."

"Tape? I'm not taping myself into a dress again," Daphne said, still fussing with her bra and the neckline of her dress. Girlfriends should get hazard pay for this.

"Unless you can do the Hokey Pokey and the chicken dance without anything escaping, you are being taped in."

"I can always let some water out," Daphne said. Anything to avoid double-stick tape. She still had gooey residue on her skin from Miranda's bridesmaid dress.

"Dance," Beth commanded.

Daphne rolled her eyes but started singing. "You put your right hand in. You put your right hand out. You put your right hand in and you shake it all about." Daphne did the motions, being especially careful to shake it all about. Rachel and Beth joined in the singing and dancing.

By the verse about putting your whole self in, Beth was singing "do the Horkey Porkey," and she literally took her whole self out by falling over the ottoman. Rachel and Daphne grabbed her arms to pull her off the floor when Daphne's bra strap snapped.

"Dolly Parton has left the building," Beth snorted between giggles.

Rachel laughed so hard she stumbled backward and fell in an ungraceful heap on the sofa.

Daphne fished around in her dress and pulled the broken pieces together. "I'm going to need some safety pins."

Rachel and Beth collapsed in gales of laughter at the word "safety."

"Just don't puncture the water reservoir or you'll be the leaky green bridesmaid," said Rachel between snorts.

## Chapter Eight

Noah pressed the doorbell again. Laughter echoed from Daphne's apartment, and it sounded like someone was singing the Hokey Pokey. If that was Daphne, she was going to love the Power Up Girls stuff he had for her. She must have visited the webpage and was already rehearsing. He shifted the folder and video to his other hand and knocked again. This time his knock was followed by silence on the other side of the door. A moment later, the door swung open.

Daphne stood in front of him, tugging up the top of her dress. She was wearing a slime green dress cut low across her chest. Each time Daphne shifted, the dress threatened to slip. He couldn't drag his eyes away, transfixed by the radiance of her skin against the fluorescent fabric. All other thoughts fled.

She gave up fidgeting with the fabric and crossed her arms over her chest.

"Hi, Noah. I forgot you were going to stop by. Come on in." She stepped behind the edge of the door and gestured for him to precede her.

With her skin out of his direct line of sight, the rest of his brain started to function again. He raised his eyes to her face. Her cheeks were flushed and her eyes glowed. Like she had just been thoroughly kissed. He wanted to give her that look. *Soon.*

He had to make up for what Aaron did. The longing to hold her would kill him, but making Daphne happy was worth it.

He stepped forward, remembering the packet under his arm. He stepped through the doorway and thrust the manila envelope toward her.

"I just stopped by to drop this off. It's the Power Up Girls stuff. The orientation meeting is tomorrow afternoon."

Daphne pushed her hair behind her ear and reached for the packet. She kept one arm across the front of her dress.

He heard giggling behind him. Pivoting on his heel, he saw Beth and Rachel sprawled on the couch. He waved and they both giggled again. Had they seen him ogling Daphne like a teenage boy? The way Beth smirked, she obviously had.

*Oh well.* Beth knew his secret anyway.

Daphne stepped around him and opened the packet. She spread the papers out on the kitchen counter. "Would you like something to drink? There's more wine coolers in the fridge, I think. Beth's had a few. Help yourself."

"No, I haven't," Beth piped up. "I'm barely halfway through this one."

Noah glanced at Beth and Rachel. "No, thanks. I'm not staying. I just wanted to drop that off," he lied.

Beth raised an eyebrow.

He'd planned to go over the packet with Daphne and see if she had any questions. Or at least use that as an excuse to hang around for a while. That plan wasn't going to work with Beth and Rachel here. It looked like they were in the middle of trying on Beth's bridesmaid dresses. *Why had she chosen such a nasty color?*

Daphne nodded as she studied the agenda for the parents' meeting.

"Hey, Noah. Did you hear the Willows burned?" Beth asked a little too loudly. "Were you there?"

"Yeah. The fire department was there all day. I missed most of Miranda's wedding and reception because of it. Hot spots kept flaring up in the afternoon heat. The chief thought sparks from a campfire Friday night may have smoldered and reignited as the sun came up on Saturday."

"Newspaper said the police were investigating. Do they think someone intentionally set the fire?" Rachel asked. "Is there an arsonist in Carterville?"

Noah snorted. "They always investigate. It's not a big deal."

"Hey, Noah, I haven't gotten your RSVP yet. I know you're coming, but are you bringing a date?" Beth slurred her words and Noah knew she was close to the bottom of her wine cooler. Beth rarely drank and when she did, it went straight to her head. Her expression said that if he couldn't come, his excuse better be more serious than his grandmother's house almost burning down. She waved a piece of paper with a bunch of circles on it. "I've got to finish my seating chart."

"Of course I'm coming. I don't have a date." He snuck a glance at Daphne, who flipped the paper over. She glanced at Beth through her eyelashes and then looked back down at the paper. "I hope that doesn't upset your plan. You can put me at the table with your elderly aunts. Then I'll have someone to flirt with." Daphne would be busy with bridesmaid stuff during the meal, but maybe he could sneak her away during the dancing. He wanted to spend some time alone with her.

"Be careful what you wish for," Rachel murmured under her breath.

Beth smirked and started to make a notation on her sheet. She stopped and chewed on the end of her pen.

"Daphne doesn't have a date either. You could come together." She drew quotation marks in the air around "come together." "I could put you two at the head table. Trust me, Noah, you don't want to listen to my Aunt Yvonne describe her colonoscopy or my cousin Ted tell an-ear-of-corn-walked-into-a-bar jokes. Besides, they both share the talent of eating like a wood chipper."

The look on Daphne's face was the same one she'd had when he'd stolen her Twinkie. He knew it well. But now it was directed at Beth. *What was that about,* he wondered. Beth seemed confused as well, but that could be the alcohol. A cotton ball could hold more alcohol than Beth.

Daphne went back to studying the papers. Noah knew she couldn't be reading anything on them as quickly as she paged through them. He stepped around the counter.

"Works for me. What do you think?" He touched Daphne's bare shoulder to get her attention, even though he knew she'd been listening.

Touching her soft skin had been a mistake. *He wanted to slide his fingers along her shoulder, down her collarbone and down along . . .*

"Sure. Whatever's easiest for you, Beth." Daphne scooted away from his touch and slid the papers back into a pile. Her fingers trembled slightly. "Leading Power Up Girls should be fun. I'll call you tomorrow if I have any questions about the informational meeting." She met his eyes, her face a mask he couldn't decipher. She shifted the papers into the crook of her arm and strode toward the door.

Noah shrugged and waved good-bye to Beth and Rachel, wishing them the best of luck with the wedding plans. When he arrived at the door, Daphne already had it open. He started through it, then leaned back toward Daphne. "I forgot to ask. How's your hand?"

Daphne blinked at him and her face flushed a deeper pink. She looked down at her thumb. She'd removed the bandage and the cut was healing in a thin red line. She held it out for his inspection. He took her hand in his and smoothed his thumb gently over the wound. It was a tiny welt on her otherwise smooth skin.

Sparks shot through him just holding her hand. What would cradling the rest of her body against his own feel like? He ached to find out.

*Damn Aaron.*

"Looks like it's healing fine. See you tomorrow." He released her hand and headed home for a very cold shower.

## Chapter Nine

Daphne closed the door behind him and slumped against it. She closed her eyes, remembering how his touch had sent shock waves through her hands and shoulder. She shook her head slightly to dispel the lingering electricity. This was so wrong.

Noah was her childhood friend, like her brother. Not a boyfriend. How was she supposed to avoid him if Beth was seating them together at her wedding? She wanted to limit their contact, not increase it. And how was she supposed to meet anyone else? If she sat with Noah at the head table, he would look like her date. Everyone would either think she was taken or trying to be a flirt.

*Thanks, Beth, for adding more complications to an already sticky situation.*

She opened her eyes to see Beth and Rachel staring at her.

"All that Hokey-Pokeying must have worn me out." She pushed herself away from the door and joined her friends on the sofa. She played with the chiffon of her skirt. "What are we going to do with these dresses?"

"We could do some kind of wrap that would tone down the fluorescence. I could make a sheer overlay of a darker green, but that would look tacky. We don't have time for things that won't work," said Rachel.

"I like the wrap idea," agreed Beth. "Then a certain bridesmaid can discard it whenever she wants someone's undivided attention." She swatted Daphne with her seating chart.

"What?" Daphne gasped.

"You saw how Noah was looking at you. You were his favorite ice cream and he wanted two scoops." Beth smiled suggestively.

"Please." Daphne shook her head, although her heart tremored at the thought he was attracted to her. "You're being ridiculous. He was probably wondering who this crazy person was who screamed the Hokey Pokey during the middle of the afternoon." She reached for her wine cooler and took a long drink. "And what's with making him my date? You know he couldn't refuse because I was standing right here."

"He wouldn't have said no anyway. Besides, you would have been the only one at the head table without a date, and I can't have my table uneven." Beth unfolded her seating chart and made a notation. "It'll look funny with four people on one side and three on the other."

"Okay, Bridezilla. Just for your seating chart, but don't make more of this than it is."

Beth arched an eyebrow in curiosity. "What more is there?"

"Nothing, and that's what I mean. There isn't anything between Noah and me. Nor should there be."

"Why not? I wouldn't kick him out of bed for eating crackers. He's attractive, single, and genuinely nice. A firefighter. How can you turn all that down? Just think of all the firefighter rescue fantasies you could act out," Rachel said, pouring herself a glass of ice water.

Daphne choked on her wine cooler. "I've seen Noah after a fire call. Grimy and stinky aren't in any of my fantasies. Although it does make me wonder about yours." Daphne grimaced at Rachel. "Why don't *you* date him?"

"Because he's not interested in married women." Beth laughed louder than normal and Daphne wondered if she should start a pot of coffee. She poured a glass of water and exchanged it with Beth's empty bottle. "I know Noah's a good friend, but good friends can be soul mates too."

Coffee was sounding better and better. Regular or decaf, she wondered.

"Jake is my best friend, and we are excellent partners." Beth winked at Daphne. Rachel slapped her hand over her eyes. "We fit together so well."

"Okay. Too much information," Daphne cut her off. Beth's common sense was soaked in alcohol and therefore useless to prevent the intimate details of her life from spilling out.

"Yeah. Save it for the honeymoon." Rachel raised her glass in a toast.

"I would lose a good friend if it didn't work out," Daphne said.

"So you're considering it?" Beth asked, downing a mouthful of ice.

*Considering it? No. Considered it. As in done. Finished. Conclusion: It's a bad idea.* What good would come of it? He would dump her and everything between them would be awkward. She'd be alone and have to go through the pain of the last two years all over again.

Not that there wasn't anything to fantasize about. Just thinking about Noah without his shirt was enough to make her mouth water. Last summer he'd coached the cross-country camp with her. He'd peeled off his T-shirt at the end of every run and jumped in the lake. He had the pectorals and biceps of Brad Pitt in *Troy*. The teenage girls on her team weren't the only ones who appreciated the view.

"I haven't given it a thought," Daphne lied.

"Sure. I believe that one." Beth attempted to stand but got tangled in the mass of bridesmaid dresses and stumbled to the side. She kicked the dresses aside and sat back down. "If you really haven't considered it, you should. You need to get out and date. Who was the last guy you dated?"

"Wasn't it the guy with green teeth?" Rachel asked.

"I still say it was spinach." Beth pointed her empty glass at Daphne.

"That four drinks wouldn't dislodge? I don't think so." Daphne shook her head.

Beth laughed.

"I think that's just an excuse to avoid a second date," said Rachel.

"He had moldy teeth. That's definitely a hygiene problem. It's a deal-breaker."

"So I'd think you'd be desperate for something better. Noah'd be just the thing."

"I was thinking about dating again," Daphne said slowly. "Just not Noah. Will there be any single guys at your wedding?" If she could divert her friends' attention from Noah, they might even help with her goal. She could avoid Noah and meet someone at the same time.

"Jake has loads of male cousins. Some of them are tall." Beth stared into space.

"Tall? Is that their only redeeming quality? Are the rest auditioning for roles as Munchkins in *The Wizard of Oz*?"

Beth snored in response. Rachel smirked.

"Could you unzip me?" Daphne asked, turning her back to Rachel.

"Sure." Rachel deftly slipped open the hook and slid the zipper down. "She may be tipsy, but she's not wrong. You need to get back out there. You can't let Aaron ruin all men for you."

"*In vino veritas,* huh? When did you start channeling Dr. Phil?" Daphne pushed the straps off her shoulders and shimmied the dress to the floor. She stepped out of the lime puddle and grabbed her T-shirt, yanking it over her head.

"I'm just saying."

"Easier said than done." She arranged the dress on its hanger and handed it to Rachel, who encased it in its plastic sheath.

Beth sat up and shook her head. She had the imprint of Daphne's couch on her cheek. "Was I sleeping?"

Rachel and Daphne looked at each other and giggled.

"I wouldn't recommend champagne for your honeymoon," said Rachel, barely containing a snort.

Beth scowled at her. "What were we talking about? Oh yeah. Jake's cousins. We'll introduce you at the reception."

Daphne nodded. "Only the tall ones. And we keep Noah out of this. I don't want to ruin our friendship."

"Just don't go running off at the reception. I saw you hiding at Miranda's wedding. You barely danced."

"My feet were killing me," Daphne insisted.

"Remember your flip flops this time." Beth glanced at her watch and shrieked. "I'm supposed to meet the caterer in five minutes. Gotta go."

"You're not driving." Rachel grabbed Beth's keys and threw the dresses over her arm. "I'll take you. You'll probably agree to having sushi or pickled pigs' feet on the menu in this state."

"I'm not drunk." Beth stood, rubbing her eyes. "I'm just sleepy and the room's wobbly."

"Thanks for the intervention," Daphne said with a hint of sarcasm. Their conversation had done nothing to settle her thoughts. What did her friends know? Neither really understood.

Going on a date with someone would be the perfect remedy. It would help eradicate the all-too-frequent thoughts of Noah from her mind. But it wouldn't be enough to keep him out completely. Her best course was still to avoid him. She'd only have to see him tomorrow at the orientation meeting and at Beth's wedding. She could tell him he didn't need to help with the Power Up Girls meetings. If she made it through those two events, she could escape seeing him until cross-country practice started in August. That should give her plenty of time to curb whatever this feeling was.

## Chapter Ten

Noah folded down the tops of his boots. He tucked his firefighter's pants into the boots and hung the suspenders from
the hooks in his locker, so they'd be ready to jump into when
the next call came. He grabbed his pager and clipped it to his
shorts.

"Hey, Banks!"

Noah turned to see Detective Ellen Widmore coming
through the doorway from the adjoining police station.

"Over here." He flipped his T-shirt right side out and pulled
it over his head.

Detective Widmore strode across the garage, looking out of
place in her crisp white shirt, black tailored skirt, and long
blonde hair. The rest of the men in the garage still wore boots or
pants from their fire protection gear and had sweaty streaks of
soot across their faces, but they all turned to watch her progress.

"Just get back?" she asked, leaning on the locker next to
Noah's. She gave him a disconcerting once over. "Biggie?"

The question caught Noah off guard until he realized she
was asking about their recent fire call. He shook his head.
"Car fire. No one was hurt, but the owner lost a pretty swanky
car. Hope his insurance was paid up."

The detective nodded, but it was obvious her mind was on

something else. "What do you make of this?" She pushed herself off the locker and held up a clear plastic bag with a charred piece of paper inside.

Noah took the bag and held it toward the light in the center of the garage. The paper was smaller than a playing card and the edges were burnt and curled. One side appeared to be glossy and dark and the other had been white.

"Looks like a photograph to me. Where'd you find it, Detective?" Noah asked, stepping back. Detective Widmore seemed to have personal space issues. He could feel her breath on his neck.

"Oh, call me Ellen. The fire at the Willows. There were a few more. Not in one place, but I'd guess they got blown around by the fire. The culprit may have been burning them when the fire got away from him. We found beer cans, too. Hard to say whether those are related to the fire or not."

"Yeah. The Willows tends to be the place to party. Can the crime lab clean it up?"

"We have to send them to the Capitol, and they're backlogged. It could be months before we hear anything." Ellen crossed her arms over her chest. Noah made a point of examining the clips on his fire coat.

"The case would be low priority for them because there isn't an insurance company breathing down their neck. I'd like to learn as much as I can before I have to send the evidence out," she said.

"They could possibly pull fingerprints, if the picture hadn't gotten soaked from the fire hoses," Noah offered.

Ellen sighed. "Soaked."

"Sorry." Noah handed the bag back to her. "Probably some teen burning pictures of his ex. Better than posting them on the Internet."

"Yeah, that's what I thought too. But look at this one." She held up another bag.

The center of the photo, presumably where the people had been, was burned away. In the upper right corner, the edge of a banner remained. The surface of the photo was blackened, but "98" could still be seen on the right end of the banner.

"Nineteen ninety-eight? I doubt any teens hanging out at the Willows would have a picture of their boyfriend or girlfriend with nineteen ninety-eight on it," Noah said. "Assuming that's what they were burning."

"I agree. Especially when I recognized the curtain in the background." She pointed a manicured nail to the edge of the picture. "Isn't that the Carterville Hornet?"

Noah glanced at the detective and then closer at the photo. "In the auditorium at the high school." He nodded. "Must be a graduation picture or something. Ninety-eight? That's when I graduated. Could I see the other pictures? Maybe I'll recognize something else."

"Great. Come back to my office." Ellen flashed him a glowing smile and sashayed across the garage.

Noah followed, ignoring the wiggled eyebrows from the rest of the department. The detective led him to a paper-covered desk behind the police receptionist. Eight plastic bags sealed with red tape topped the stacks.

"We found ten pieces. No faces on any of them." She waved her hand at the bags.

"Well, that would have made it too easy."

"No kidding." Ellen leaned her hip on the edge of her desk. Her skirt slid up, exposing a rose tattoo on the side of her thigh.

Noah kept his eyes focused on the evidence bags. If he didn't know better, he'd think the detective was flirting with him. She was pretty in a leggy blond sort of way that did nothing for him. She was too aggressive. She didn't have Daphne's creative spirit and enthusiasm.

He pointed to one of the bags. "I can't say a hundred

percent, but this could be my prom. The silver tree thing looks familiar."

"So that narrows it down to—what? Three hundred people who went through Carterville High in the late nineties?" She slid off the desk and bent to look at the picture.

"Maybe less. Not everyone still lives around here. About half moved away after college." Noah stepped around the desk. He picked up another bag and made a pretense of looking at it in the light from the window, just to get her out of his personal space.

"Do you know if the spot had special significance to anyone?" she asked.

"Any teenager who used to hang out there. But I don't think that narrows your suspect pool either."

## Chapter Eleven

Daphne spent the morning stuffing T-shirts and tie-dyed bandanas into plastic bags for the Power Up Girls orientation, and directing volunteers and sponsors in setting up the meeting room. She grabbed the last box of bags and carried it over to the sign-up table.

Yvonne taped a poster board to the front of the table and stepped back. "All set."

Daphne dropped the box next to the others. "That looks good. Yvonne, could you make sure the mics are working? I don't want to have dead batteries."

Yvonne nodded and headed for the stage. Daphne pulled her bandana out of her pocket and tied it around her hair. She tucked her Power Up Girls T-shirt into her shorts, smoothing down the billowing fabric. She'd grabbed an extra-large to save the smaller sizes for the girls, and the T-shirt was huge. She glanced at the clock and pushed the play button on the CD player. The opening beats of "Girls Just Wanna Have Fun" echoed through the speakers.

Yvonne tapped her on the shoulder. "PA system's ready to go. Anything else you need?"

"Thanks. Could you check with the sponsors and see if they need anything?" Daphne asked, and Yvonne hurried off.

By the second verse of the song, mothers and daughters

started trickling in. Daphne greeted them at the door and directed them to the sign-up sheets in the center of the room and the various booths around the perimeter.

"The face painter needs some water and paper towels," Yvonne said. "What should I do?"

Phyllis had engaged the Ladies Night Out Social Club to help with setting up. The Ladies were sweet and well-intentioned, but caused more work than they completed. "There's paper towels and cups in the supply closet. You can get water from the bathroom."

Yvonne hurried to the hallway as fast as her orthopedic sandals could carry her.

Daphne turned to greet the next arrivals and found a young girl in tears. Daphne knelt beside her. "What's wrong?"

"My dad left me," she said between sniffles. "He didn't see any other dads here. It's all moms."

"There are a lot of moms here," Daphne said, patting the girl on the shoulder. "But dads can come too. Do you want me to see if I can catch him?"

The girl nodded. Daphne took her over to the face painting table and reassured her she'd be back with her dad.

Daphne walked out of the meeting room, then sprinted down the hallway to the parking lot. She scanned the rows of cars, but didn't see the girl's dad. Had he already left? She glanced at her watch. She didn't have time to track him down. The presentation was supposed to start in a few minutes. She jogged the length of the parking lot and headed back to the meeting room, trying to decide what to tell the little girl.

As she approached the door, she saw Noah climb out of his truck.

"Just what I need," she called. Noah waved, a smile growing on his lips. She grabbed his arm and ushered him inside. Sensation rocked through her as she felt his muscled forearm under her fingers. She pushed the feeling away. "I need you to be a dad. This girl's dad ditched her. Didn't even help her sign up."

Daphne pulled him over to the little girl, who now had a rainbow on one cheek and a butterfly on the other. "Noah's going to help you out. He'll get you signed up and make sure you have everything you need. Okay?"

The little girl nodded at Daphne and beamed up at Noah. Noah grinned back and extended his hand. She took it and they headed off to the registration table.

Yvonne managed to find the needed supplies and deliver them to the face painter, so Daphne posted her at the door to direct the late-comers to the sign-up table. Daphne headed toward the raised dais on the far side of the room.

Daphne took a deep breath and released her microphone from its stand. She spoke in front of people all the time, but in a new situation the butterflies returned. Daphne scanned the audience of eager young girls and their mothers. A few dads populated the crowd as well. They looked uncomfortable sitting cross-legged on the floor in the sea of women.

"I'd like to welcome everyone to the Power Up Girls orientation. I'm glad to have so many girls here at our first meeting." She scanned the crowd, recognizing the parents of some of her students and the younger siblings of the girls on her cross-country team. "It's great to see so many moms and dads here today with our girls. I would like to . . ." Her eyes lost focus for a second when she saw Noah leaning against a pillar with the little girl's hand tucked in his. He wore a crisp white T-shirt that accentuated his muscled chest and biceps. "I'd like to thank our sponsors for all the fun things they've brought for us today. The T-shirts, bandanas, balloons, and much more. Let's give them a hand."

The crowd clapped politely and Daphne used the moment to collect her thoughts. Noah *would* have to stand directly in front of her. It was almost impossible to make eye contact with the audience and not see him. She took a slow cleansing breath and looked only at the front row. She'd advised her speech students to imagine the audience in their underwear to help them overcome nerves, but that wouldn't work in this situation. She refused to make eye contact with anyone more than halfway back in the room, so she wouldn't accidentally catch Noah's eyes. If she did, the only thought in her brain would be *Boxers or briefs?*

"The Power Up Girls program is going to be great for Carterville. We want to encourage self-esteem and self-respect in our preteens. The program is designed to do that in all aspects of their life and especially encourage them to keep it up for many years to come. We do this through running. Well, not only running, but that's a big part of the program." She caught Noah's eye and he grinned. And she'd lost her train of thought again. She hoped whatever she said made some sense to the audience.

"Running has never been about winning races and going fast for me. It's about challenging myself to work hard and remain dedicated to keeping myself healthy. We hope to instill the same values in the girls here today. We want every meeting to be upbeat, and so, as the girls arrive, we will be playing girl-power music." Daphne cued another one of the Ladies to turn on the music.

"We want you to be excited about being here and to be active as soon as you walk in the door. So let's start dancing right now." She gestured for the girls to stand up. They got up slowly, looking around the room. A couple of moms jumped right up and started the clucking motion.

"There's nothing to be embarrassed about. How can you be embarrassed when everyone is doing the chicken dance?" Girls giggled at their moms and dads, who reluctantly flapped their arms and shook their tailfeathers. The dads' motions started small, but when they saw the excitement on their daughters' faces, they got into the dance as well.

Daphne's gaze strayed to Noah's pillar. He looked as if he were trying to *become* it. The little girl looked his way expectantly and he hesitantly clapped his hands offbeat.

She couldn't resist laughing to herself. *So that was why he didn't want to lead the meetings.* Now that she thought about it, she'd never seen him dance at their high school parties and only the obligatory dollar dance at weddings. That was it.

She would love to tease him about this. She kept watching him as they skipped and twirled; he was always one beat off. His awkwardness was kind of cute.

Maybe she could make one exception in her resolution to avoid him. She could tease him about this and leave it at that. One little conversation as they were cleaning up after the meeting and that would be it. She'd go home, take an ice bath, and go back to avoiding him. Until Beth's wedding.

No, she should keep her distance and not play with fire.

*But he's a fireman,* Rachel's words whispered in her head. He could make playing with fire safe.

Her gaze found him with his arm hooked through the little girl's arm. They skipped in a circle, then released arms and reversed direction. The young girl smiled up at him as her ponytail bounced behind her. Noah grinned down at her, one dimple etching his cheek. The little girl looked as if she'd found her white knight on his gallant steed.

Daphne felt the same look creeping onto her face. He looked so adorable.

*Okay, one quick conversation.* She could hold it together for five minutes.

The music ended with the girls laughing, some still shaking their behinds. Noah followed the little girl in clucking his hands, flapping his arms, and wiggling his tush. The little girl hugged Noah and he wrapped his muscular arms around her. Daphne's breath caught. *What would it be like to have the excitement of that little girl? To have Noah's arms around her?*

She caught herself before her fantasies wandered too far down that path. She allowed herself five minutes to make fun of his skipping and the conversation would be over.

"That's how we kick off all our meetings. I hope you can't wait to come back. I'd like to thank everyone for coming. I encourage all the girls to bring a friend to our next meeting. Be sure to check out our sponsors' booths before you leave. They have lots of goodies for the girls. Power Up Girls is so much fun!"

The crowd flocked to the booths surrounding the room and Daphne breathed a sigh of relief. The first meeting was over and everything had gone smoothly. If only she hadn't been concentrating on Noah for more than half the meeting.

"Daphne, what would you like me to do now?" Yvonne called to her from the stage stairs.

Daphne thought for a moment. "Collect all the leftover packets and put them in one box. Then pack up the PA system, but wait to do that until most of the crowd is gone. I'd like to keep the music going."

Yvonne gave her a thumbs-up and headed for the registration tables.

Daphne didn't run into Noah until the crowd had cleared out. She tipped a table and folded the legs against the bottom.

"Let me help you with that." Noah grabbed an end of the table and they carried it to the storage closet.

"I don't think I've seen a chicken dance quite like yours," she said, as she kicked the wedge under the closet door to prop it open.

"You know I don't dance." Noah balanced the folded table on its end and pushed it into the closet.

"I thought you were just being a party pooper. You dance

like a drunk chicken." She mimicked his awkward steps. "Doo dee doo dee doo dee doo, doo dee doo, dee doo doo," she sang.

Noah laughed and hooked his arm through hers. They skipped in a circle and he twirled her around, exaggerating his inability with lumbering steps. "Like this? It's how it's done at all the weddings."

Despite the jostling of their dance, heat flushed through her where his skin touched hers. Suddenly, she felt tipsy. She should have left him alone.

"You probably haven't seen anyone dance it sober," she said breathlessly.

He laughed. "You're probably right. And since the only models I've had for dancing are drunks, I'll stop." He did immediately. Daphne continued skipping and almost crashed into his chest. She caught herself with millimeters to spare.

Noah reached out to steady her, but she stepped back before his hand made contact with her arm. Her pulse throbbed. Any doubt about what she felt for Noah was washed away. Attraction burned in her blood.

*Ice cold bath, ice cold bath,* she mentally repeated. She unhooked her arm from his. She edged back toward the meeting room. "I better go check on Yvonne. I asked her to pack up the PA system."

"You what? You know she steals batteries," he called after her.

She scurried over to the stage and busied herself with disassembling the microphone stand and packing it into its padded box.

She couldn't trust her feelings. She couldn't trust her actions. Now her nerves were singing. She knew teasing him would be a bad idea, but she had done it anyway. She needed to keep a tighter rein on herself until her attraction to him wore out. She'd betray herself in a minute if she didn't.

"Ice cold bath," she whispered to herself, and goose bumps popped up on her arms. At least that suggestion was working. She snapped the microphone case shut and stood up.

Noah grabbed the suitcase from her and swung it into his arms. "You want to grab something to eat?"

Daphne untwisted the support on the microphone stand and pulled the two pieces apart. "I've got . . ." she paused, trying to think of an excuse. "I've got Beth's bachelorette party. Maybe another time."

She couldn't spend time with him right now. She needed that cold bath. At least she had enough wedding errands for the next couple weeks to come up with plausible and legitimate excuses. She didn't trust herself to keep it platonic. She knew she'd be watching him for signs he felt more than friendship, and she didn't want to do that. No, it was better to let whatever attraction she'd felt at Miranda's wedding die, and then she and Noah could go back to being friends again.

## Chapter Twelve

Hey, Noah," Jake called, as Noah jumped out of his truck at the beach parking lot. Noah waved and grabbed a folding chair from his truck bed, before heading toward Jake and his brother, Ray. They and the four other guys invited to Jake's bachelor party hovered around a blackened grill. A picnic table held the steak packaging, a stack of paper plates, and a box of plastic silverware. The guys lounged in folding chairs around the grill. Beach towels and sandals were tossed in a pile on the bench of the picnic table, although no one looked dressed for swimming.

"How's the water?" Noah asked.

"Too cold for water polo, too hot for ice fishing," Ray said, shaking Noah's hand and slapping him on the shoulder. "Which means it's just about perfect." He winked and Noah nodded.

"Glad to see you're back in town. New office treating you well?"

"Not bad. Not bad. Lot of old people in town want their wills done." Ray steered Noah toward the grill. "Beer's in the tub there. Steaks are about ready." Jake nudged a piece of meat closer to the fire with the oversized tongs. Juices sizzled in the flames.

Noah swiped a damp can from the slush-filled tub and popped the top open. He unfolded his lawn chair and joined the rest of the guys.

"You think you can play with fire just 'cause it's your stag party?" he called to Jake.

"You're here now. It's safe." Jake grabbed a bottle of lighter fluid off the picnic table and pretended to spray it into the coals. "Fire up the barbie."

Noah laughed. "I'd prefer my steak juicy, not crunchy, thank you."

Jake rolled his eyes and tossed the lighter fluid on the table. He looked back at the grill. "These are about done. Hand me those plates."

Noah grabbed the stack of paper plates and peeled them apart. He held one out for Jake to plop a thick juicy steak on it. The plate caved dangerously under the weight.

"Do you have any of those wicker things to put under these?" Noah asked. "You can't put steak on these flimsy ones." He peeled five plates off the stack and layered them under the first one.

"They were the cheapest," Ray said.

As Noah passed the plates around to the other guys, making sure to give each of them a hefty stack, he realized he'd attended all their weddings within the last year. Except Jake's and Ray's, but then Jake's was on Saturday.

When would his turn come? His career was going well. He'd found the woman he wanted to marry. The woman he wanted to have children with. He wanted to settle down. Why couldn't he get the last piece of the puzzle to fall into place?

He'd waited for the right time. It felt right now. If only Aaron hadn't ruined everything. Would he ever get a chance to talk to Daphne? He wanted to fulfill his dreams with her, but he didn't feel any closer than when he was in ninth grade.

Noah stepped over the bench of the picnic table and sat down. "What else is there to eat?" he asked, as he sawed at his steak with a plastic knife.

"I knew I forgot something," Ray said, as he thunked his

beer on the table. "I was going to pick up some potato chips."

"You need a keeper," Jake said, as he stabbed his steak. The plastic tines of his fork bent without piercing the meat. "Maybe we can find one for you at the wedding."

Ray laughed sarcastically. "My ankle's just fine without a ball and chain." He jogged to the convenience store across the street with a warning to the others to leave his steak alone.

"Like we could do anything to it with this wimpy silverware. We couldn't saw a piece off before you got back," Jake called after him.

Ray returned after a few minutes with two bags of potato chips, a bag of beef jerky, and some pork rinds. *Yum.* Noah could feel his arteries clogging.

Ray dropped the bags in the center of the group and dove into his steak. He stabbed it with two forks and held the whole sizzler up. He ripped off a piece with his teeth.

"Nice," Jake said, dutifully hacking away. "Were you raised in a barn?"

"It's all guys here. Who cares? Live it up while you can, little bro."

*I'm tired of living it up,* Noah thought. *I want more out of my life. I want someone to share it with.* Nights out with the guys were becoming less and less appealing.

"Or are your ankles already shackled? Does that scare the crap out of you, Jake? Being tied to one woman for the rest of your life?" Ray asked.

Jake chewed a piece of meat thoughtfully. "I'm not nervous about that. I'm more worried I'll forget one of the things Beth wants me to do, and she'll be ticked off at the wedding."

"She's letting you take care of something? I thought she knew you better than that," Noah said, grabbing a bag of chips and tearing it open. He poured a handful on his plate, trying to ignore the grease stains already dotting the paper.

Jake raised his eyebrows and shrugged his shoulders. "Beats me."

"What's she got you doing? Picking up pantyhose?"

Jake shook his head. "I have to tie ribbons on the programs. My fingers are too fat for tying little bows." He waved his hand in the air. "I had them all done and Beth took one look at them and had a hissing canary. The bows were lopsided. I have to do them all over again. Oh, and I've got to come up with some game thing."

"Game? For what?" Noah asked.

"The reception, I think. Something about the clinking glasses. The country club doesn't allow it, so she left it to me." Jake took a swig from his beer. "I got nothing."

"You better think of something if you want to kiss your wife at the reception," Noah said. "That's what she's talking about. You better hurry, you only have three days."

Noah wished he was planning his own wedding. He'd hate tying ribbons and listening to highbrow music and getting fitted for a tux, but in the end it'd all be worth it. To see his bride walking up the aisle toward him, glowing in white. Lifting her veil and kissing her. In his dreams it was always Daphne.

"Oh." Jake smacked his palm against his forehead. "I had no idea. I just nodded and smiled like I always do when she talks about wedding stuff. She'll kill me if I don't come up with something."

"I was at this wedding once where they had goldfish on the table and you had to eat one for them to kiss," Ray said. "Not the crackers, live fish."

"That's baloney." Noah waved his fork.

"Seriously. One guy tried it and choked. It was disgusting. Someone had to give him the Heimlich." He slapped his chest with his beer can and beer shot out of it, splashing in his lap. "Crap." He snatched a beach towel off the ground and wiped at the wet spot on his shorts.

"You could take a collection," Ray said. "When a table gets fifty bucks together, you kiss."

"My family's too cheap. We wouldn't get fifty cents."

"You could have the guests answer trivia questions about you guys. If they get it right, you lock lips."

Jake scratched his head. "That's a possibility. Beth would like it."

"She would, but you'd have to come up with thirty questions," Noah reminded him.

Jake's face fell.

"And have the right answers."

Jake swore under his breath. "I'm screwed."

"I was at a wedding where they had an envelope on each table with instructions. They had to do what was in the envelope to get the couple to kiss."

"He'd have to come up with thirty things again," Noah said.

"Not going to happen. I need something that requires no effort."

"You could have each table sing a song with the word 'love' in it. They'd have to come up with the song and sing it," Noah said. "You'd only have to make sure there was an available mic."

"I like that." Jake nodded slowly. "Beth will think it's cute too." He finished the beer and chucked the can in a box of empties. It rattled against the others. "Don't let me forget what it is tomorrow morning," he said, popping open a can of soda.

"Where are we all sitting, Jake? Beth didn't split us up, did she?" one of the guys asked.

"Hope you're not next to Uncle Jared. That man has gas." Ray pretended to choke.

"She put you all together, except Noah. There wasn't enough room at your table so he's at the head table," Jake said.

"Well, la di da," Ray said, pointing his nose in the air. "Get to sit with us snooty folks, eh?"

"She told me she needed to even out your table because

Daphne didn't have a date," Noah said, leaning forward. The look on Daphne's face when Beth suggested it still puzzled him. It was as if sitting next to him was the last thing she wanted to do. He had no idea why. He couldn't recall offending her, but she'd been treating him strangely since Miranda's wedding.

Jake shrugged. "All I know is there's eight places at the tables, and these four and their wives will fill it up. Speaking of Daphne, when are you asking her out?"

Noah barely swallowed his beer before it shot out his nose.

*If it wasn't for Jake's wedding,* Noah thought, *I might have had two dates with her.*

"You got a thing for Daphne?" Ray asked, slapping Noah on the back. "She's cute, I guess. Hey, Jake. You could set us up. I'd let her be my keeper."

*I'd keep her away from you,* Noah thought.

"Well, Noah's sitting by her at the reception, so he's got first dibs," Jake said.

*Dibs? Like she was a jelly doughnut?*

"Yeah. Whatever." If she ever sat down. At Miranda's wedding, she was so busy with bridesmaid stuff, he'd barely spoken two words with her. At every wedding, she ran around taking care of this and that. He wouldn't get more than five minutes with her.

She'd be wearing that green dress her skin glowed in. He'd be mesmerized by it. He wouldn't be able to concentrate on what she said. He'd have to remember to request the Hokey Pokey from the DJ. A grin curved his lips just thinking about it.

Ray punched him in the arm. "What dirty thoughts are in your head?"

Noah wiped the grin off his face. "Anyone want the last piece of steak?" he asked, sticking it with his fork. "Oh, I guess it's mine now." He slid the meat over to his plate and attempted to dissect it with his plastic silverware.

*Or the chicken dance.* He merged the image of her in the

bridesmaid dress with her shaking her behind at the Power Up Girls meeting. He didn't need any lighter fluid. Daphne had him flaring up and she wasn't even here. *What if he touched her silky skin or kissed her?* His hands itched to cradle her, to press her body up against his.

He'd spontaneously combust.

Then he had an idea. He jammed his fork in the steak and the tines snapped off.

"Whoa there, Hulk." Jake laughed. "Don't know your own strength?"

"Feats of strength," Ray growled, flexing his arms in an exaggerated pose.

"I was at this wedding once where every time the bride and groom kissed, they had another couple at the wedding kiss. Her parents, his parents, grandparents, the wedding party, and so on," Noah said.

"We left that conversation ten minutes ago."

"I'm just saying." He chucked his broken fork on the table and fished a new one out of the box. He scratched at his steak with his plastic knife, hoping no one noticed how red his face grew. He must have daydreamed for a while; he hadn't heard a word they said.

Jake rolled his eyes. "I'm cutting you off. When you can't keep up, you can't drink anymore."

"Fine." Noah looked at the sky. The sun was edging to the horizon. "I think it's about that time." He looked around the group. The other guys nodded.

They rushed Jake and threw him up on their shoulders. He protested half-heartedly, knowing it was inevitable. They'd all had their turn, except Noah, and Jake had been the instigator. They ran down the beach and toppled Jake into the water. He splashed beneath the waves and came up sputtering. He scrambled through the water for his baseball cap as it rolled on the surf.

Noah laughed and snatched the cap out of the water. He flung it toward one of the other guys after wading farther from the shore. The cool water eased the tension in his body better than the cold showers he'd been taking.

The guys roughhoused in the water, playing keep-away with Jake's cap until the sun set. Eventually the guys scrambled out of the water and rubbed themselves down with their towels before heading home to their wives. Ray said something about people to do and things to see and jumped in his convertible. He waved as he sped out of the parking lot.

Noah and Jake looked at each other and at the table strewn with cans, meat wrappers, chip bags, and paper plates.

"I'll haul a trash can over here so we can clean this up," Jake said.

Noah shoved the debris into a pile and pushed it into the can Jake propped at its edge.

"She's the one, isn't she?" Jake said, fitting the lid on the trash can.

"Who? Daphne?" Noah asked, faking indifference.

"Who else?"

"I've been shot down twice." He shrugged. "And what about Aaron?"

"What about him? He's an idiot. What else is there?" Jake glanced at his watch. "Crap. I've got to finish the ribbons on the programs tonight. You want to help?" He wagged his eyebrows.

"You make it sound so tempting. No, I'd rather clean up this mess."

## Chapter Thirteen

Why is Peggy wearing a costume in all these pictures? Are they all Halloween?" Noah flipped through a stack of pictures and tossed them on the table. He leaned back on the couch and propped his foot on the coffee table.

Daphne plopped down on the sofa near him, careful to leave a safe distance between their bodies. One large enough so she wouldn't accidentally brush against his warm skin. She had been reluctant to agree when he asked for help picking out pictures for Peggy's slideshow. Avoiding him seemed to be the best option for sorting out her confusion between him and Aaron. Once she had the two men straight in her mind, then she could comfortably spend time with Noah. As aware as she was of the heat emanating from his body, she knew she wasn't there yet.

Unfortunately, she'd been the only dork dragging the Polaroid camera to every event, and had taken hundreds of pictures. Plus, she was a sucker for looking at old pictures and knew finding ones of Peggy would be fun. She thought she could endure an evening of sorting pictures if she kept their physical contact to a minimum. But her heart had started thudding as soon as she spied him through her peephole.

"This is Peggy, remember? Every day's a costume ball." Daphne pulled the lid off a shoebox and thumbed through the contents. "It's a shame you can't choose who you're related to. Peggy's my only female cousin and we're the same age, so we were forced to do everything together. Dance class, trick or treating, you name it. Peggy's fun and all, but she's always over the top. It takes a lot of energy to keep up with her. Luckily, one Peggy is enough for Carterville, so no one wanted me to be like her."

"I wish that had been the case with Aaron. But then people always got us mixed up, so they'd congratulate me about things he'd done. It felt like I was in his shadow, even though the things people praised me about weren't things I wanted to do." Noah pulled a picture out of the stack he was flipping through and tossed it on the coffee table, then slid the rest back in the envelope.

"I never understood how people got you two confused. You look alike, yet your attitudes and actions are completely different."

Noah shrugged. "You probably just noticed because we were all together all the time. You could see us side by side." He picked up a picture from another stack and stared at it. "I always thought he and Peggy should get together. Like he'd chosen the wrong cousin. They both always want the spotlight on them. I mean, not that I wanted him to dump you . . . you know what I mean. I thought you could do better than Aaron."

Daphne slid a shoebox from under the coffee table and lifted the lid. "Peggy and Aaron wouldn't have worked. Neither could share the spotlight. That's probably why Aaron and I stayed together so long. I didn't detract from his adoring public." She handed Noah a glossy photo album. "There might be some middle school pictures in here."

"She's wearing an Elvis in Vegas costume." Noah squinted at a picture on the first page of the album. "Look at the hair. Is that a wig?" He leaned toward her and brushed against her shoulder.

"Yep. Picture day. The principal made her take it off for her official photo." Daphne reached for her soda and took a long sip, willing the liquid to soothe the flush on her skin.

Noah agreed. "A miniature Elvis wouldn't work so well if they needed the picture for a missing child photo."

"But then, who would kidnap her?" Daphne glanced at the picture. "She did all those rhinestones herself. She is the only person I know who wore out their Bedazzler."

"Bedazzler?"

"It was absolutely fantastic. You could stick rhinestones on anything. I did a pair of jeans. Put 'Daphne' across my butt."

"I don't remember those. Did you ever wear them to school?"

"My mom wouldn't let me. I think they ended up in the Goodwill pile. Sitting on rhinestones is not fun." Daphne extracted another envelope and winced. "Prom."

"Peggy at prom? I've got to see those. What was her theme?" Noah reached for the envelope.

"You were there. You're in all these pictures, even. See?" She pointed to a figure on the edge of the photo. "Right there. You don't remember?" When Noah shook his head, Daphne said, "*Men.* You don't remember anything important."

"I remember your dress was lavender." His voice was low and quiet. It took him a moment to look up at her. When he did, Daphne lost herself in his blue eyes. There was a message there she didn't want to identify. It wasn't nostalgia or disappointment, but it felt like a little of both, and with her conflicted emotions about him, she shouldn't want to pursue it. Yet, the look on his face still broke her heart. She ached to pull him close to her. To feel the scratch of stubble along his chin on her cheek.

She caught herself before she leaned closer. She fake-coughed and reached for her soda, chastising herself for this dumb idea. Spending an evening reminiscing about high school with Noah ranked at number one. Talking about Noah and

Aaron and all their adolescent exploits was only convoluting her emotions. She needed to straighten herself out.

*Why would he remember what dress she wore?* Then she saw pictures in his hand. "You don't remember anything. You just saw the photograph." Some of her anxiety eased. Poor Noah, now she was projecting her own emotions on him.

"No, I remember. It had a criss-cross ribbon thing in the back." He drew *x*'s in the air. "And you could see—" He stopped, pink flushing his cheeks.

She playfully punched his arm. "What? You could see what?"

He looked away from her. "Never mind. Got any more pictures of Peggy?"

"Never mind nothing. You could see what?" She pulled her legs under her, kneeling beside him on the couch.

He glanced at her and rubbed his forehead.

She gave him her best teacher look. It worked on her students every time. She wasn't disappointed.

He rolled his eyes and sighed. "You could see the tan line from your bikini through the ribbons."

Daphne leaned away from him, laughing. "You remember that?"

Noah shrugged. "It stood out."

"It better not have. Beth put so much sunless tanner on me, her hands turned orange. She had to wear full-length gloves."

"There were definitely strap marks. Maybe you should get your money back. You can probably see them in the pictures." Noah made a show of studying the picture in front of him.

*He noticed her tan lines?* Somehow that felt very intimate. Like he knew what was inside her, the things she only shared with close friends. Then she realized Noah had always seemed to know what she was feeling, and she couldn't remember ever telling him. He was just there when she needed him.

*What if . . . ? Oh crap! What if he knew she was attracted to him?* She cast a sidelong glance his way. He had resumed leafing through the pictures. Daphne pushed a loose curl behind her ear and contemplated the ceiling. *Just focus on the task at hand. Pretend like there is nothing else besides these pictures.*

"I think junior prom was during Peggy's Goth phase. Maybe Morticia Addams." She leaned closer to Noah and peered at the pictures.

*Sandalwood and woodsmoke.*

Her nerves shivered again. She inched away. *Task at hand,* she reminded herself. *Task. At. Hand.*

"There. Aunt Becky had a conniption over the neckline of her dress."

Noah pulled the picture closer. "Is that her belly button?"

Daphne pulled the hem of her shirt down at the mention of belly buttons and finished off her soda. She placed the can on the coffee table and edged away from Noah. She needed space to regain her senses.

"Uh-huh. That was the first time I heard of using double-sided tape to hold your clothing in place. It also explains why her Goth phase was closely followed by the Laura Ingalls phase." She handed him another envelope of pictures. "Ruffles, poke bonnets, and petticoats. All at the senior prom."

"She looks like Little Bo Peep," Noah said, skimming through the pack without removing them from their envelope.

"Oh sorry. That's homecoming." Daphne chose another envelope. "Here."

"Weird. How many pictures do I need for this slideshow thing?" Noah pulled a couple of photos from the pack and tossed them on the coffee table.

"About seventy-five total. I've got more of Dustin around here somewhere." Daphne reached for another shoebox. "How did you get roped into doing it anyway? I thought Dustin's brother was going to put it together."

"His computer got struck by lightning. I volunteered." He closed the envelope and tossed it on the coffee table.

"That was nice of you."

"I didn't realize how nice. Can I just pick pictures randomly?" He reached for his beer on the side table.

"There's kind of a formula for it. A couple of baby pictures of the bride and groom. A picture or two of them doing something funny as toddlers. Really dorky pictures from middle school. Skip high school unless they were dating then. Then fill the rest in with pictures of the happy couple. How'd these get in here?" Daphne extracted an 8" × 10" and a handful of wallets from the shoebox. One glance at their subject and the sickly feeling oozed through her. Aaron.

"I thought I got rid of all these," she muttered, throwing the pictures on the floor. They slid in a fan shape below the coffee table.

Noah leaned over the edge of the couch. "Hey, I'm in that one." He pulled the pictures toward him with his fingertips. "This is our whole group. Can I have these? I don't have any pictures from high school."

"Sure, whatever. I'm trying to purge Aaron from my life in every way I can. If only I could burn away the memories as easily." She tossed the box on the floor and headed for the closet.

"No problem." Noah flipped through the pictures quickly, then set them on the arm of the couch. "Wait a minute." He grabbed the top photo. "These are our prom?"

"Yeah." Her last, really good big occasion with Aaron. The last time he was the big fish in the little pond. After that, he was always trying to prove something to the new crowd he was trying to join. How fast his car was, how much money he made, or how sexy his girlfriend was. It irked him every time she didn't overdress—or underdress, actually—for their dates. At first, it was flattering that he wanted to show her off. She worked hard to keep in shape and she appreciated his notice. But then she realized his notice wasn't because of her hard work, it was because the other men would give Aaron a thumbs-up. Like he had anything to do with the miles she ran and the sit-ups she did every night.

"They found some partially burned photos at the Willows. The same decorations are in them. These might help in the investigation."

"No kidding. Someone's burning our pictures from our prom? I don't blame them. Tacky decorations and fashion disasters." She pulled a photo album off the shelf and walked back to the couch. "Here we go. Baby pictures of Peggy." She plopped on the couch and handed the album to Noah. He flipped it open.

"Are you sure? This kid is wearing normal clothes." Noah leaned closer to Daphne. His shoulder brushed hers.

Her skin sizzled. Tonight was supposed to prove she could behave as if they were friends. No blushing. No rapid heartbeats. No missed breaths. It wasn't working. Avoiding him was her only option.

## Chapter Fourteen

Is Detective Widmore around?" Noah asked the uniformed officer at the reception desk.

"She's in the shooting range." The officer jerked his thumb to the stairway.

Noah waved in thanks and headed down the stairs. He grabbed a pair of headphones off the wall before he pushed the door open. The report of gunshots greeted him. He clapped on the ear protection and closed the soundproof door behind him.

Ellen stood in front of him, her feet planted shoulder width apart. The recoil rolled through her shoulders with each shot. The acrid sulfury smell burned his nose and he rubbed it absently. The detective removed the magazine from her gun and cleared the chamber. She put the gun on the counter in front of her and removed her ear protection. He tugged off his own and approached her. She shoved her safety glasses on top of her head and pressed the button to bring her target forward.

"Nice cluster," Noah commented, as the target came into view. A circle of torn paper surrounded what would have been the culprit's heart.

"Thanks. You planning to shoot?" She brushed a strand of hair out of her face.

Noah shook his head. "You have any leads on the Willows fire?"

"You know I can't comment on an ongoing investigation." She winked at him. "But I might make an exception for you."

"I may have something that will help." Noah pulled the photos from his pocket. "My friend had these." He hesitated on the word *friend*. *Was that really all Daphne was to him?* It seemed like there should be another word to describe her. *Best friend. Girlfriend.* He wished.

Ellen stood next to him, almost too close. Noah leaned away from her and against the partition of the shooting booth, trying to escape the powdery fragrance of her perfume. He handed her the photos and she flipped through them quickly, nodding. She repeated the process more slowly, studying each picture.

"You haven't changed much," she said, stopping on the last photo. "Well, maybe you're a little more muscular now. You lift weights now?"

"Occasionally."

"It shows." She looked at the group photo. "Are you still in contact with all these people?"

The photo included Daphne and Aaron, Beth and Jake, Max and Miranda, Peggy and Dustin, and Noah. Noah listed off the names for the detective, stumbling on the married names of the women. "This guy is Aaron Banks. He doesn't live in town anymore."

"Banks? Is he related?" she asked. "I can see the resemblance."

"Cousins. We aren't close." Noah couldn't keep the edge out of his voice. He crossed his arms over his chest.

"Anymore, I take it. He has his arm across your shoulders." She studied him, her eyes narrowing.

Noah glanced at the picture. Aaron's other arm cradled Daphne's waist. Daphne looked so happy. Of course, Aaron was still treating her like the Homecoming Queen. "Things change. We haven't spoken in over a year."

The detective crooked her finger toward him. "Come upstairs with me."

Noah followed the detective to her office. Once there, Ellen pushed her door closed and opened a cardboard box marked EVIDENCE with a case number written in permanent ink below it. She extracted a plastic bag and reclosed the box. She held the burned photo and the whole one next to each other and compared them.

"I think these are the same photo." She showed them to Noah, standing next to him and allowing her hair to brush his shoulder.

"Looks like it to me. The people are all burned out of the one found at the fire, but you can see part of Peggy's skirt here." He shoved the picture toward her and edged around the chair in front of her desk. He felt like he was being hunted.

"Do you know who else had copies of these photos?"

"Probably all the girls. Maybe the guys too. I just got this one from Daphne. She said it was her last one."

"What happened to her others?"

"She said she got rid of them." Noah scratched his head, not liking the direction this conversation was going.

"Do you know who took the picture?"

"That one's the professional photographer's. Daphne was usually our group photographer."

"Hmm." Ellen wandered around her desk and sat in the chair. "Could you write down the names and contact information of everyone in the photo?" She shuffled through the papers on her desk for a pen and a pad of paper.

Noah sat in the chair in front of her desk and started writing. "You think someone in the photos was destroying the pictures and the fire got away from them?"

"You got it. I know they're your friends, but do any of them have any reason to burn these pictures?"

Noah's thoughts flew to Daphne. She mentioned getting rid

of everything that reminded her of Aaron. And wanting to burn the memories as easily.

*Could she have set the fire intentionally? Burned all remnants of Aaron in her life? She and Aaron spent a lot of time at the Willows. Was she trying to destroy another memory of Aaron?*

*No.* He couldn't see Daphne taking a lighter to the pictures. Watching them turn to ash was too passive. Daphne was active. She probably shredded them. Watching the little blades of the shredder gnaw the pictures into shreds would have been more her style.

"Most of the couples are married to each other or will be shortly." He pointed to Aaron and Daphne in the photo lying on the desk. "Except these two."

"Broke up?" Ellen picked up the photo and tapped it against her hand.

"Yeah. It was pretty ugly." *To put it mildly.* What Aaron did to Daphne was like a late hit in a football game and a kick in the gut for good measure. He treated her like a trophy to show off, then he cheated on her. When he finally dumped her, he didn't even have the guts to do it in person. Aaron had called her like he was running late for a date. He said he wouldn't be picking her up for the family reunion and, by the way, he'd like to see other people.

He and Noah had stopped speaking then too. Noah couldn't believe his own flesh and blood could treat someone like that. Noah left the space on his list next to Aaron's name blank. He didn't know or care where he was.

"How long ago was the breakup?" Ellen made some notes on the page of addresses.

"Over a year."

"Are they still in the area?" She clicked her pen and shoved it through the spiral of the notepad.

He winced, wishing the signs pointed somewhere else. "Daphne is."

"Well then." She flashed him a look like a cat who ate the canary. "I know who to question first."

"Daphne didn't set the fire."

Ellen stood and came around her desk, her movements slow and almost predatory. "And how do you know that? Were you with her?" She tossed her hair over her shoulder.

"No. She wouldn't do something like this. It's not Daphne." He thought she'd been at Miranda's, getting ready for the wedding, but they weren't sure exactly when the fire was set. It could have smoldered for hours before anyone noticed it.

"Not Daphne?" The detective propped her hip against the desk. "How well do you know Daphne Morrow?" She glanced at her notepad as if she needed to check the last name, but Noah doubted she did. "Is there more to your history you're not telling me, Noah Banks?"

She almost purred his name. Noah shifted uncomfortably in his seat, then stood up to put more space between them. The rest of the fire department had teased him about Detective Widmore having the hots for him, but he didn't believe it until now.

"Daphne's a good friend," he said, leaning back and bumping into the door.

"You're in love with her, aren't you?" Her eyes narrowed and her voice turned colder. He expected her to jab him in the chest with her finger, as if loving someone was worthy of accusation.

"That's none of your business." He pushed his shoulders back and stood up straighter.

Ellen put her hands on her hips. "It is my business if you're covering for her."

Jerking the door handle, he said, "Daphne didn't start the fire. It's not creative enough."

"But she had motive. A woman scorned isn't a person you want to mess with. They can do unexplainable things." Her face darkened and Noah saw the threat there. He let the door swing shut.

"Daphne wouldn't burn the pictures. She'd cut Aaron's head out of them and do something crazy with them."

"Like what?"

"I don't know." He threw his hands up in the air. "Glue them to pictures of donkeys and leave them on his doorstep. She wouldn't burn them." He looked straight at the detective.

She turned away from him and walked back around her desk. She shuffled a couple of papers on her desk into her folder. "Okay. But I'll have to talk to her anyway. She did have a copy of the picture. She may be able to help."

Noah nodded and left. That conversation hadn't gone like he'd imagined. He should probably warn Daphne the detective would be coming.

## Chapter Fifteen

Daphne wiggled her shoulders under the lace shawl they decided would lessen the glow of the fluorescent green bridesmaid dresses. Unfortunately, the lace kept sliding off her shoulders and it itched.

Beth and her groom were gazing deeply into each other's eyes as they recited their vows. Daphne tried to listen to what they were saying. They had written their own vows without the usual "for richer, for poorer." But she couldn't concentrate. Beth had wanted them to stand so they partially faced the audience, and Daphne could see Noah out of the corner of her eye. He'd said hi before the wedding started and she'd dropped her bouquet. Luckily, only a couple of petals had been crushed.

Ever since, she'd felt as if an electric wire connected them in the stuffy sanctuary. How was she supposed to get through the rest of the evening with this hyper-awareness of his presence? She mentally shot a dark look at Beth for placing him at the head table next to her. The rest of the evening would be like playing Operation—any move too far in one direction or the other would set off a buzzer that frayed her nerves. She was already buzzing, and he was across the room. *Focus,* she chided herself. *You're supposed to be concentrating on the wedding.*

"You may kiss the bride," she heard the minister say, and

she jerked her attention back to the happy couple entwined in an extremely passionate embrace.

She heard a cough from the audience, but she refused to look at Noah. Sure, he'd won the bet, but he didn't have to rub it in.

"I would like to present Mr. and Mrs. Jacob Maloney." Rachel handed Beth her bouquet. The couple almost skipped down the aisle, Beth's face glowing in happiness.

Rachel stepped forward and grasped the arm of the best man. Daphne followed and took the arm of the remaining grooms-man and proceeded down the aisle.

Many of Beth's aunts wiped tears from their eyes with embroidered handkerchiefs, but Daphne's eyes strayed to Noah. He sat about halfway back on the groom's side. Daphne had wondered which side he would choose to sit on, having known the bride and the groom for several years. He wore a crisp white shirt with blue pin-stripes and a blue tie. The white glowed against his tan skin. In fact, he appeared rosier than at the Power Up Girls meeting. He must have been at a fire yesterday. A telltale lighter streak around his eyes hinted at the shape of a face mask.

He tilted his head toward the woman next to him and his mouth curved into a grin at something she said. He nodded to Daphne as she walked past.

Something green twisted itself inside Daphne, but she plastered her grin on and faced the bride's side of the church. What reason did she have to feel jealous? Noah wasn't hers and she didn't want him to be. She joined the receiving line and smiled and greeted guests until her cheeks ached.

Beth and Jake departed for the reception in a horse-drawn carriage. The rest of the wedding party was driving themselves so they didn't have to return to the church to retrieve their vehicles.

Daphne collected her clothes and makeup from the dressing room. Throwing her duffel bag over her shoulder, she dug in her purse for her keys. Head down, she walked into something hard.

*Noah.* She recognized the cologne. His hand on her back steadied her. Her breath hitched as she realized she was practically in his arms. Actually, there was no practically about it. His arm circled her waist and held firmly against her back.

She stepped back and his touch slid across her waist and dropped away.

"I thought we could ride together," he said, as she wrapped her fingers around her keys.

"Why?" It was the first thing that popped into her head and she kicked herself as soon as she said it.

He gave her a perplexed look. She shook her head slightly and said, "I'm sorry. I meant, aren't you on call this weekend? Don't you need to have your own vehicle available?"

Noah shook his head. "The guys let me off this week for covering last weekend. Besides, I need to collect my winnings."

Daphne popped the clasp on her purse and withdrew a ten-dollar bill. She handed it to Noah.

"Well, that was disappointing. I was hoping you'd take it from your winnings."

"Huh?"

"Your, um . . ." His face turned bright red. He tapped his chest.

"Very funny." Daphne rolled her eyes and headed for the car. He tossed her duffel bag in the backseat and folded himself into the passenger side of her Honda Civic. Daphne climbed into the driver's seat and tried to untangle herself from the shawl. Noah helped her, and chills ran down her spine when his hand touched hers.

*Why hadn't she said she was riding with someone else?* She couldn't seem to avoid Noah no matter how hard she tried.

She tossed the itchy shawl into the backseat and jammed her key in the ignition. Warm air poured out of the vents. She quickly punched the buttons on the dash for the air conditioning. After a few moments, cool air flooded into the car and Daphne shifted into drive.

She forced herself to concentrate on driving and the traffic around them rather than Noah's muscled forearms as he unbuttoned the cuffs of his shirt and rolled the sleeves up to his elbows. She pushed the fan lever over to high.

Noah cleared his throat. "We had a good response from the Power Up Girls registration. Several more girls signed up after the orientation."

"That's great," Daphne said, turning the car onto a shortcut to the country club. "The girls seemed excited. I hope it makes a difference for them and for the community."

"I'm just glad you agreed to head things up. I thought I could do it until I found out about the dancing and the meeting about 'becoming a woman.'" He shivered. "I never look forward to talking to the boys."

"That's why I teach English literature. You don't have to deal with it as much. Occasionally I get questions from the cross-country team, but it's not too bad."

A rattling noise came from under the hood of her car that sounded like someone beating a cowbell with a hammer.

"What's that?" she gasped, her fingers gripping the steering wheel. "Is that my car?"

"I think it is," Noah said, rolling down his window. "You'd better pull over." Daphne maneuvered the car to the shoulder and threw it into park. Noah was already stepping out of the car and walking around to the front.

"Pop the hood," he called.

Daphne fumbled under the dashboard for the release and gave it a quick jerk. The hood popped an inch and Noah bent over to find the latch.

"Do you want me to turn off the engine?" she called, as he propped the hood. The sound grew louder. Whatever it was, it didn't sound good.

"Not yet."

Daphne climbed out of the car. Noah stood with his hands on the metal piece above the grill and surveyed the engine compartment.

Daphne looked as well, but saw nothing unusual. No belts dangling loose, no tube with a gigantic hole in it, no big arrow pointing to what was wrong. Most everything was metal gray or black with grease.

Noah stuck his fingers against something in the right corner of the compartment. He leaned into the sun and studied the residue.

"Antifreeze," he muttered and turned back to the engine.

The rattling sound clattered unevenly. "Go check your temperature gauge."

Daphne went to the driver's side door and peered through the window. "It's not in the red yet. Is it something with the radiator?"

"I think it's your water pump. It's still pumping, but it's got a leak. There's water and antifreeze sprayed everywhere. It's probably going to break completely soon. How far is the reception?"

"About fifteen miles."

The rattling stopped.

"Turn off your engine. The pump just died."

Daphne climbed into the car and twisted the ignition off. "What are we going to do now?" she asked, poking her head out the door.

Noah continued to unscrew caps and peer into containers under the hood.

"Do you have any water?" he asked, coming around the

side of the car and holding his grease-covered fingers away from his white shirt.

"I think I have a couple of bottles in the trunk. Leftovers from the orientation." She reached beside her seat and punched the trunk release. The hatch popped open.

Noah retrieved the bottles from the trunk.

"The radiator level is low, so your engine will seize if we drive too far. If we add water and crank the heat, we should be able to make it back to the church without the engine overheating. We can switch cars and come back for yours tomorrow."

Daphne sighed and attempted to push her fingers through her hair, but realized that the beautician had shellacked every strand into a solid and unmoving mass. Wait, she thought, she had her cell phone.

"We could call a tow truck. Then we wouldn't have to worry about the car overheating," Daphne said, as Noah poured the water in the small hole at the front of the engine compartment. She reached for her purse.

"It'd take an hour for the truck to get here. We'd miss the reception," he said, taking a drink from the last bottle before pouring the remainder into the car.

Daphne nodded, knowing she didn't want to ruin Beth's day with a missing bridesmaid. She climbed in the driver's seat.

Noah removed the hood prop and slammed the hood shut. He wiped his hands on a rag and tossed it in the trunk, shutting it. Then he walked around to the driver's side of the car.

Daphne reached for her seatbelt and snapped it across her lap.

"I could drive," he said, through the open door.

Daphne reached for her keys and shook her head. "Just tell me if I need to do anything different."

Noah nodded and walked around the car and folded his

body into the compact's seat. Daphne started the car as he flipped all the levers on the heater to "hot" and "high."

"Keep an eye on the temperature gauge. If it gets into the red, pull over right away."

Daphne executed a perfect three-point turn and drove back toward the church.

"If we break down, we won't need road flares. My dress will catch people's attention."

Noah laughed.

They made it back without any further mishaps. The temperature gauge rose, but the car did not overheat.

At least the engine didn't.

With the heat cranked up all the way and Noah brushing against her shoulder to check the gauges every few seconds, the interior of the car felt like it was two thousand degrees. She was surprised her hairdo hadn't spontaneously combusted with the gallon of hairspray caked on it.

She'd have to remember this beautician for any beach weddings she'd be in. Nothing seemed to move a tendril of hair. Daphne wondered if this hairstyle might be permanent.

The heat of the car intensified the fragrance of Noah's aftershave, and it intoxicated her.

She breathed a slow sigh of relief when she pulled into the church parking lot and was able to get a reprieve from Noah's overwhelming presence.

Noah helped her grab the things she needed from the backseat and loaded them into his truck. As soon as they were back on the road, Daphne dug in her purse for her cell phone and informed Rachel she'd be a bit later than planned. Rachel knew what to take care of, and the rest would wait until Daphne and Noah arrived.

Daphne tried not to think about what she would have done if Noah hadn't been with her. She'd have called a tow truck and waited for them to arrive and missed the reception. She cast a sidelong glance at him as he maneuvered his truck out of the parking lot.

*Why hadn't she ever noticed how cute he was until Miranda's wedding?* She had plenty of friends she could set him up with. If she found someone else for him, then her attraction to him wouldn't ruin their friendship. She could keep herself in control if she knew he was attached to someone else.

Then she remembered their conversation at Max and Miranda's. *Wasn't he in love with someone?* No, he didn't say that. He said it was complicated. Maybe she could help him fix the problem and then he'd be off limits.

They arrived at the country club with just enough time to arrange the bows and flower arrangements around the terrace leading to the reception hall.

Noah remained by her side the entire time, helping to attach the flowers to the posts. Her fingers fumbled the bows and the wires as if she had an extra set of thumbs on each hand. By the time they finished, Daphne was desperate to get away from the tangy scent of his aftershave and his unsettling presence.

## Chapter Sixteen

Noah loosened his tie and unbuttoned the top button on his shirt. After the overheated drive with Daphne, the pool on the other side of the garden called to him. He thanked the waiter who refilled his water glass, then downed the entire contents, filling his mouth with slivers of ice.

It had taken all of his willpower to keep his fingers off the tiny beads of perspiration glowing on Daphne's neck. Every time he leaned to check the gauges, he caught the scent of lavender. He tortured himself by checking them every half mile just to keep the scent of her perfume fresh in his nose.

The DJ announced each of the attendants, and Noah's gaze strayed to Daphne as she giggled at something her escort said. Noah rolled his eyes. The man never once looked at her face. Not that Noah blamed him. Despite the color, Daphne was breathtaking in that dress, but Noah liked the whole package.

Daphne didn't seem to notice. In fact, she encouraged the groomsman by bumping his shoulder with her elbow. From his vantage point across the room, Noah could see her skin shimmer.

*If only Aaron hadn't started dating her. Noah could have asked her out long ago. They might even be married now.*

Flirting with the groomsman was the first indication Noah had seen that Daphne was ready to move on. He'd better act quickly before someone else attracted her attention. Like the short dweeb in the monkey suit.

The DJ announced Beth and Jake, and the rest of the wedding party promenaded through the hall to the head table. He joined the procession at the table with the rest of the significant others and followed Daphne to their seats. He pulled her chair out for her and bent forward to inhale her perfume as he pushed the chair forward. It was all he could do to keep his lips off her tanned skin.

She turned to thank him and his face was mere inches from hers. His gaze dropped to the luscious redness of her lips. Her breath caressed his cheek.

Glasses clinked and guests hooted. A rustle of satin and tulle next to him reminded him where he was. He quickly took his seat, as Jake bent Beth over his arm and kissed her thoroughly.

After releasing Beth, Jake gestured for the microphone.

"To save the crystal, we'd like each table to come up with a song with the word *love* in it. Everyone from the table has to come up to the mic and sing it."

Daphne's attention jerked to Beth, who had commandeered the microphone "We'll pull the name of a couple from this box each time, and that couple has to kiss too."

Daphne sighed. "Thank goodness my name's not in there."

Beth pulled the first card from a decorated box and announced her parents' names. They stood, laughing, and placed chaste kisses on each other's cheeks and lips and then blew kisses to Beth and Jake.

Noah reached for a fresh glass of water and tossed the contents down his throat. He was going to need a lot more ice to get through the evening. Especially if Jake and Beth kept steering his thoughts and Daphne was within reach.

The minister offered a prayer. Then the master of ceremonies directed the tables toward the buffet, laden with ham and cheese, croissants and strawberries, pomegranates, and grapes.

Noah was the first to stand when their table was directed to the food.

"Hungry?" Daphne asked, pushing her skirt out of the way.

"Always." He grinned.

"That's probably why you agreed to Beth's ridiculous offer. You knew you'd be the first to eat."

"The thought didn't cross my mind," Noah acknowledged. He hadn't thought about anything but Daphne since she'd walked down the aisle.

They loaded their plates and returned to the table. Beth and Jake had barely set their plates down when a group of guests crowded around the microphone. They attempted a rendition of "Love Is in the Air." The cacophony of their singing was worse than the clinking glasses.

Beth and Jake less-than-dutifully stood and kissed. Beth drew a card and announced an aunt and uncle to follow their lead. Beth and Jake had barely returned to their seats when the aunt and uncle commandeered the microphone for "I Need a Lover."

"That song shouldn't qualify. It's 'lover' not 'love,' " Daphne said.

"I don't think Jake cares," Noah said. Daphne shrugged her shoulder and turned back to her food.

"Who came up with this dumb idea anyway?"

"As a matter of fact, I did. You're jealous you didn't think of it first," Noah said, as Beth's grandparents approached the microphone.

"Congratulations, Beth and Jake. Hope you are as happy as we are." Granddad moved the microphone in front of Grandma, and she started to sing, "Love and marriage. Love and marriage . . ." The tune was almost recognizable as the theme from *Married with Children*.

"Only twenty-eight tables to go," Daphne muttered under her breath. "Beth hasn't taken more than two bites of her food yet. She spent hours deciding on the menu. If I get married, I'm going to have hot dogs and paper cups."

Noah spoke close to her ear. "I don't think she cares about the food."

A blush rose up Daphne's neck and flooded her cheeks.

She was rescued from replying by Jake's friends commandeering the microphone. They launched into "Brown-Eyed Girl" with more gusto than knowledge of the lyrics. They mumbled along off-key until they got to the chorus.

"I wonder if they know the word 'love' isn't until the third verse." Daphne swiped a carrot through her dab of ranch dip.

"Hey, I'm just glad I'm not sitting at that table," Noah said when the singers finally arrived at the necessary word.

Daphne laughed. "All that and they flubbed the line."

Beth and Jake kissed anyway, and named Jake's parents to follow suit.

"What do you mean 'if'?" Noah asked when the microphone had been vacated.

"If what?" Daphne asked, setting her glass back on the table. Noah's gaze strayed to the pink lipstick along the edge.

" 'If you get married.' Don't you think you will?" He dropped a half-eaten carrot stick on his plate.

Daphne shrugged. "My Magic Eight Ball said, 'All signs point to no.' " She laughed, but Noah could tell it was forced.

"Daphne, I'm serious. Don't you think you'll get married someday?" He shifted to face her. If she was giving up on relationships, his chances were sunk.

"To whom? Men aren't exactly lining up to ask me out. And ever since Aaron, I don't know, I haven't wanted to put myself out there again. It took so long to get over him. Maybe I'm better off single. I could get a few cats."

"Be the crazy cat lady? I think you're more of a dog person." Noah glanced around him.

"We should sing the Oscar Meyer weiner song."

"What?"

" 'That is what I'd truly like to be.' Come on." She shoved her chair back so quickly, it caught on her dress. He heard the chiffon rip, but Daphne barely noticed. She rounded up the rest of the table and herded them over to the microphone.

Noah followed reluctantly, wondering how Daphne got him into these things. They belted out the song, singing like children at a Christmas pageant, more or less yelling at the top of their lungs. Ray clutched his heart as if the only thing he ever wanted to be was a hot dog.

Beth and Jake stood and clapped. Then Jake bent Beth so far over his arm, Noah expected them to both tumble to the floor and roll under the table. Ray whistled and Rachel yelled, "Get a room!"

The rest of the group wove their way back to the table. Beth pulled a card from a basket and announced another uncle and aunt.

Noah and Daphne took their seats. Noah picked up his fork and leaned toward Daphne. "This probably isn't the best place to say this, but I think you should take the chance."

" ' 'Tis better to have loved and lost than never to have loved at all,' " she replied.

"Yeah, something like that. You've already lost once. The pain can't be as bad the second time."

"Spoken as only a male could. Especially one who's never dated anyone seriously."

"Touché. I think we have a golden opportunity here." He smeared a cube of cheddar into the ranch dressing and popped it into his mouth. "We could go—"

"Noah and Daphne!"

"What?" Daphne gasped. He saw the flush from the sun drain to white and her mouth fell open.

If she was that horrified, his chances were definitely sunk.

Beth grinned at them. Jake peered around her and winked at Noah. Out of the corner of his eye, he saw several expectant faces among the guests.

"You can kill Beth later," he whispered, as he tugged her to her feet. "For Jake's sake, after the honeymoon."

He leaned toward her and feathered his lips across hers, silently thanking Jake for this opportunity.

The electricity of the contact rocked him. Everything he expected it to be and much more. The temptation to pull her closer, to deepen the kiss, almost overwhelmed him.

He just barely held his compulsion in check.

Reluctantly, he allowed Daphne to pull away. He sat down and held her chair for her. She sat, grasping for her water. He saw a large chunk of ice slide into her mouth. Her chest rose and fell in deep heaving breaths.

*Hmm. Maybe she wasn't horrified.*

## Chapter Seventeen

Leprechauns with naughty suggestions and a bathtub full of packing peanuts were too good for Beth. Daphne's hand trembled as she placed her glass on the table. This required Vaseline and plastic wrap on the toilet seat revenge.

She pointedly ignored Beth's amazed stare as she picked at the food on her plate. Not that she could swallow anything.

*What had Beth been thinking?* Daphne had specifically eliminated Noah from any matchmaking attempts. *Where were all these "tall" cousins of Jake's?* Her ice melted too quickly to ease any of the fever. She gulped another mouthful.

Eventually the throbbing of her heartbeat eased and she could focus on what was happening at the reception. She pushed her plate away, sneaking glances at Noah. He was leaning back in his chair, talking to Rachel's husband.

Obviously, the kiss hadn't affected him in the same way it had rocked her.

She couldn't use him to replace Aaron. She wanted to keep her relationship with Noah platonic. As it had always been. But their situation was making it harder and harder. If she didn't avoid him, she'd do something she would regret and lose a friend because of it.

Ray and Rachel made toasts to the newlyweds and then they danced their first dances. Luckily for Daphne, when the bridal party joined them, she was partnered with the other groomsman. Not one of the tall cousins either. His forehead came to her jaw and she knew his gaze never went above it. He was holding her so close his five o'clock shadow scratched her décolleté. The safety pin on her bra strap dug into her skin, and she hoped it didn't pop open, stabbing her or her water reservoir. The groomsman squeezed tighter and she briefly wondered what kind of pressure her water bra could take.

The gush of water between her breasts answered her question. She gasped as the water flooded down her chest and soaked through the front of her dress.

"I'm sorry," the groomsman said, attempting to blot the wet mark with the sleeve of his tux. All he succeeded in doing was dislodging her dress from the deflated bra. The groomsman stood close enough that he could undoubtedly see down to her navel. She would have been able to see it herself if his head hadn't been in the way.

She snatched at the now gaping neckline and fled the dance floor. Once in the ladies' room, she inspected the damage. Wriggling out of the top of the dress, she removed the soaked bra. Holes gashed both reservoirs. She dried the bra as well as she could with paper towels, then eased it back on.

Her dress was another story. Although little could make the fluorescent green worse, a watermark down the front did the trick. Without the pint of water, the neckline of her dress sagged limply, exposing more of Daphne's breasts than she felt comfortable showing to Jake's non-tall cousins.

She'd have to wear that infernal itchy shawl the rest of the night. She blotted the excess water from her dress and contemplated stuffing some wadded paper towels in her bra to fill it out. She tossed the paper towels in the garbage before she could seriously consider the thought. The bridesmaid business was getting to her, if she could even consider walking around like an underdeveloped adolescent.

Daphne yanked the bathroom door open, planning to head straight for her shawl, when Noah pushed himself off the wall across the hallway.

"You okay?" he asked. "I was hoping we could talk."

*What was he thinking?* She didn't want to talk about the kiss or her wardrobe malfunction. She'd prefer to pretend neither of them had happened. Her mouth opened and closed as she searched for an excuse. She turned to see Beth dragging a good-looking man toward her. He was actually tall.

"I've got to grab my shawl and talk with Beth. Maybe later?" She gave him a half smile, then dashed down the hall, holding her dress on her shoulders with a death grip. She retrieved her shawl and wrapped it tightly around her shoulders. She tied a puffy bow over her chest and hoped it camouflaged the wet, saggy front of her dress.

"Daphne, what happened to your dress?" Beth asked, pulling a face.

"You don't want to know." She crossed her arms over her chest to hide the largest watermark. "Who's your friend?"

"This is Michael." Beth introduced the man hovering behind her.

Michael held out his hand and Daphne shook it. He wasn't unattractive. Lean, clean cut, but nothing special. He asked her to dance and she followed him to the dance floor.

"I'm glad they went for the open bar," he commented.

Daphne thought she heard a slurp before he spoke. She brushed it aside. Maybe he was enjoying the open bar and slurred a little bit. She was being picky.

"What do you like to do?" she asked. He may not be drop-dead gorgeous, but he was cute, and after the midget, she deserved a dance without the threat of whisker burn on her chest.

*Slurp.* "I collect things. Mostly movie memorabilia."

He did it again. Now she knew she hadn't imagined it. Maybe he was . . . Maybe what? What explanation could there be? Too much saliva? An extra drippy nose? *Eww.* Definitely a deal breaker.

"You must have some really cool things. What's your favorite?" she asked, figuring she should at least finish the dance.

"Hmm. That's a tough one." He looked down at his shoes. "I'd have to say my opening night *Star Wars* ticket."

"Ticket? What's that?" She glanced around for Beth so she could give her a dirty look, but saw Noah instead. He raised an eyebrow, and she turned so she couldn't see him. She was avoiding him. Michael wasn't that bad. He was a collector. Heck, she had an entire shelf of first edition books. They had something in common. It was a start.

"I have every ticket stub from every movie I've ever seen." He nodded like this was a major accomplishment.

*Or not,* she thought.

"Every movie?"

Michael spun her, and she saw Noah heading toward them.

"I've taped them to my bedroom wall. It's difficult to find acid-free tape that adheres to painted surfaces, but after hours of searching I've found something that works well. I only have a square foot left before I have to start on the hallway."

Daphne wondered how desperate Beth thought she was. You couldn't get much lower in the barrel than Michael.

Noah tapped Michael on the shoulder. "May I cut in?"

Michael blinked from Noah to Daphne and back. "Okay. Could I get your number?" he asked Daphne. "I'd like to show you my collection."

Daphne couldn't have been more thrilled when the DJ announced the bouquet toss right then.

"Oh, I better get ready," she said, stepping away from Michael and Noah. "It was great hearing about your collection." She turned and hurried toward the crowd of single women congregating on the other side of the dance floor.

*Was he Beth's idea of a joke?* Wait until Beth returned from her honeymoon, she'd find out what a joke really was. Daphne hadn't been saving all those life-size cardboard NASCAR drivers for nothing.

Daphne wormed her way to the back and tried to maneuver taller women in front of her. Beth winked at Daphne over her shoulder before she tossed the bouquet. The bundle of flowers tumbled her way. Daphne hefted Beth's little cousin and shoved her in its path. The little girl clutched the flowers—after they hit her in the face—grinning from ear to ear. Daphne patted her on the shoulder and wandered off the dance floor.

The DJ called all the bachelors for the garter toss. A whole crowd of men ambled onto the dance floor. A chair was brought for Beth, and Jake made an elaborate show of crawling under her skirt and removing the garter with his teeth. He waved it above his head. The men wolf whistled and cheered. Jake spun the bit of pink and lace around his finger.

The DJ played a drumroll and Daphne's gaze found Noah, standing toward the front of the group all shoving and jostling for position.

Jake shot the garter into the masculine mass like a rubber band. A familiar arm snatched it out of the air. The crowd parted and Noah stood with the garter stretched around his tanned fingers. Several of the men clapped him on the shoulder and arm. He just grinned.

The DJ announced that the winners of the bouquet and garter tosses would lead the next dance. Daphne watched the color fade from Noah's skin faster than the water had leaked out of her bra. She hurried over to the DJ and suggested the perfect song for their dance.

The DJ shuffled through her CDs and slipped Daphne's suggestion in the player. Daphne grinned to herself as the first notes of the "Chicken Dance" rolled out of the speakers. Noah rolled his eyes but extended his hand to the little girl, who was already flapping her arms and shaking her tail feathers. She grinned up at him and grabbed his hand. As they skipped around the dance floor, Noah caught Daphne's eye.

"Thanks a lot," he mouthed as he passed by.

Daphne shrugged her shoulders and pretended not to understand him. Noah waved for her to join them, but Daphne shook her head. Then the DJ echoed his sentiment and called for everyone to dance. Beth rushed to the dance floor and pulled Daphne by the arm.

Noah's dancing skills hadn't improved since the Power Up Girls meeting, and Daphne hoped the videographer was still filming. She had to admit, he was cute and loveable, just not for her.

As she danced along, Daphne realized the torture of an immovable hairdo. Her head ached. She could feel each and every bobby pin poking into her head. Daphne would need to "lather, rinse, repeat, lather, rinse, repeat" to restore any bendablity to her hair. It'd be easier to shave her head.

Thankfully, Beth and Jake were leaving after this song and she could go home.

Daphne retrieved the baskets of bubble canisters from behind the bar and, after handing a basket to Rachel, distributed the bubbles to the guests. On the DJ's cue, the exit from the reception hall was clouded with the iridescent orbs. Beth and Jake strolled through the corridor of guests, waving and giving hugs as they went.

Beth's eyes glowed and her cheeks were flushed. Jake grinned from ear to ear. Even as he turned to hug his brother, Ray, in a one-arm hug, he kept his other hand at Beth's back.

Jealousy stabbed at Daphne. Beth was so happy and Daphne wanted nothing less for her. But when would it be her turn? Her turn to have someone look at her like there was no one more beautiful in all the world. To carry her as though she weighed nothing. To hold her as if she was more precious than crystal.

As Beth and Jake exited, they kissed and waved to the guests one last time before climbing into their limo. Daphne waved and chucked her canister of bubbles into the nearest trash can. It made a satisfying thud against the metal. Her last duty as bridesmaid at this wedding, and now she could retreat to her home and a warm bath.

Exhaustion didn't begin to describe how she felt. All the activity and the emotional tilt-a-whirl had worn her out. Waving to Rachel and her husband as they left, she made a beeline for the head table where she'd stowed her purse. She dug in her purse for her keys.

"Damn," she hissed, remembering her overheated car. She'd have to hitch a ride. A quick survey of the room found the munchkin groomsman, Mr. Ticket Man Michael, and Noah. None of whom she was eager to be confined in a vehicle with. Maybe she could catch Rachel.

She kicked off the silver sandals she'd crammed her feet back into and ran out of the reception hall, hitching her skirt in lime green handfuls. By the time she reached the parking lot, Rachel had left. Ray exited the hall with a woman draped on his arm. The woman stumbled against him, and he filled his arms with her.

Nix that idea.

She shoved open the door to the hall and scanned the room again.

"Daphne?" Noah approached from the bar. His shirtsleeves were rolled up to his elbows, revealing muscled forearms. "Were you looking for someone?"

Despair and excitement warred within her. Noah was the last person she wanted to talk to right now, but her skin tingled in his presence. She fidgeted with her shawl, adjusting the bow. Then realizing what she was drawing attention to, she dropped her hands. Should she make something up and hide in the ladies' room until he left? The number of guests still at the reception was dwindling along with her chances of finding another ride. "I was getting ready to go home."

"Great. I want to get out of here too. The music is getting to me." Noah pulled the door open and Daphne had no choice but to walk through.

"You're just afraid they'll play the 'Chicken Dance' again."

"Yeah, and I saw you talk to the DJ."

"I thought that was your song," Daphne said as she clambered into the truck cab and piled the fluorescent chiffon on her lap. She wedged her purse next to the console and dropped her shoes on the floor. "It shows off your natural grace."

"Only if I'm dancing with someone under five feet tall." He turned the key and the engine rumbled to life.

A smile curved Daphne's lips. He'd made that little girl's day. Just like at the Power Up Girls meeting. Those two little girls would adore him forever. Kind of like how she felt. If she didn't know better, she'd think she was falling for him.

Except she wasn't going to let it happen.

She leaned her head back in the seat and heard her hair crunch. She reached up and inched a bobby pin loose. One down, two hundred to go.

Thankfully, Noah was concentrating on the winding turns on the dark road and leaving her to her thoughts. He didn't say anything until they reached the lights of town.

"I can come over and fix your car tomorrow."

"No, that's all right." Daphne dumped a handful of pins into her lap. "I don't want to take up your whole day."

"It's no problem. It should be easy to fix. I can pick up a new water pump and install it in the morning, then we'll be off to the beach in the afternoon."

"The beach?" Daphne gasped, as she lost hold of a pin and yanked a strand of hair instead.

"Yeah, so we can talk." Noah pulled over in front of her

place and shifted the truck into park. "Let me help you with that." He reached across the cab and touched Daphne's hair. It was all she could do to keep her seat. Just the thought of him touching her hair had her reaching for the door handle.

"Just relax." Noah slipped the pins out one by one, but her hair remained stubbornly in place. He wove his fingers into the shellacked mass and drew the locks gently apart, caressing her scalp with each touch. He traced his fingers down her neck and across her shoulders, tantalizingly along the edge of the lace shawl.

Daphne shivered. Goose bumps swelled and her skin felt tight against her damp dress.

*So this was avoiding him, huh?* In another second or two, there wouldn't be any space between them.

"Damn," Noah murmured. He dropped a bobby pin and it slid down the front of Daphne's dress. "Where'd that go?"

He fumbled for the overhead light. Daphne snapped her seatbelt loose and shoved the door open. Light flooded the cab and she slid out of the truck. The cool night air yanked her out of the seductive fog.

She pushed her hair over her shoulder and bolted for the safety of her apartment.

"Wait. Daphne?" Noah pushed open the door and stepped out.

She turned back at the bottom of her steps. Noah's figure was silhouetted in the light of the truck. And she saw Aaron. The shape of his face. The angle of his shoulder.

The urge to grab a rock from her driveway and hurl it at him overwhelmed her. She pictured herself winding up and pitching rock after rock. Hearing the metallic twang as they bounced off the pickup. She gripped her shawl until the lace dug into her shoulders. She inched backward, giving herself distance.

Noah slammed the door shut and Daphne jumped, recognizing Noah again.

She'd never confused Noah and Aaron this easily before.

*Why was she letting her old feelings for Aaron resurface? Was she imagining reactions from Noah?*

If anything, she knew her perceptions and emotions couldn't be trusted. What she needed now was time and space to sort it all out.

Noah approached, gently placing his hand on her arm. She felt the warmth through the scratchy lace. "Are you okay? You look like a little deer caught in the headlights."

"Just a little disoriented." She tried to laugh it off. His body was close to her and she could feel the heat emanating from him. "Must be the champagne. I'm getting like Beth. I'll be fine. Just need some sleep."

His hand slid to her shoulder, and he looked down at her. He worked his lower lip as if he wanted to say something more. "I'll call you tomorrow about the car." His hand disappeared, and she missed it.

She climbed the stairs and pushed her door open. She stopped inside the doorway and looked down at Noah, waiting at the bottom of the steps. She raised her hand in a wave and Noah returned it. He watched her for a moment and then returned to his truck. The engine roared and he backed out of the driveway. She allowed her screen door to swing shut, barely conscious of the snagging sound her dress made as it caught on the torn screen. She watched Noah's taillights disappear at the corner, and she could have sworn his pickup morphed into a cherry red Camaro.

## Chapter Eighteen

The next morning, Noah's trip to the auto parts store took him past Beth and Jake's new house, and what he saw in the driveway caused him to slam on his brakes.

Daphne's blue Civic sat in the driveway with the trunk wide open and a piece of cardboard sticking out of it.

"What the . . . ?" He pulled into the driveway and parked behind her car. After everything they'd gone through yesterday with limping the car back to the church, she should have known not to drive it.

He jerked open the screen door and stopped halfway through the doorway.

Daphne stood facing a cardboard cutout of Jeff Gordon, twirling a white thong with red lipstick prints on it around her finger. She wore a T-shirt and shorts that highlighted her toned body, and her ponytail swayed as she contemplated the figure before her. Cardboard Jimmie Johnson, Kasey Kahne, Greg Biffle, Bobby Labonte, and Carl Edwards lounged against the kitchen counters.

He was satisfied when she jumped as the screen door screeched. A pained look crossed her face, but was quickly replaced by a veneer of surprise. She snatched the thong and wadded it in her fist.

"What are you doing here?" she asked, glancing down at

the pile of colorful silk and lace on the table beside her. Several thongs were pinned to suggestively shaped potted cacti.

Noah crossed his arms over his chest and leaned against the door jamb, not allowing the door to shut.

"Your engine blow yet?" he asked, trying not to clench his teeth.

Their eyes met and Daphne's mouth moved to say something, but no sound came out. She closed her mouth and licked her lips.

The slight glimpse of her tongue dissipated his irritation for a moment and cleared his mind of any thoughts but the image of her glistening lips. He tore his gaze away.

"I called the shop and they had the right part. They fixed it this morning."

Noah clamped his keys in his fist until the jagged metal cut into his palm. *Didn't she believe he could help her? Was she trying to avoid him?*

"I said I could fix it." He stepped inside and let the door close behind him. He'd imagined working on the car while she lounged in the sun next to the driveway. They would talk. He'd explain how he felt about her and how he wanted to make her happy. She'd look at him and smile. She'd say she felt the same way, but didn't know how to tell him. She'd rush into his arms and they'd kiss. . . .

Daphne hesitated. "You did? I guess I forgot." She looked down, reaching for the pile of underwear. "I wasn't altogether with it last night. Must have been the champagne or something. I could have sworn I saw . . ." She scrunched up her forehead, then rubbed the wrinkles with her still-manicured fingertips. "Never mind. Anyway, I needed to get Beth's welcome home present done today. They're supposed to be home tomorrow."

She turned to face Jeff again and snapped the thong around his baseball cap. She draped a leopard print one over his outstretched hand. Then she picked him up, carried him to the living room, and stood him next to the television.

"Short honeymoon," Noah said, as he leaned against the archway that divided the kitchen and living room.

"Uh-huh. Jake doesn't have any vacation yet at his new job, so they're going to take a cruise at Christmas. Since you're here, you can help me get these guys set up. Could you run out to the car and get Dale, Jr.?" She scowled at the cardboard cutout and removed the thong from its head. "I want him and Jeff next to the television."

Noah moved closer. He didn't want to run her errands right now. She wasn't going to dissuade him from speaking. "Daphne, we need to talk."

"About what?" She scooted past him and back into the kitchen. She absently sorted the thongs into color-coded piles. She flicked a sheer candy-apple red one across the table. It slid away from the intended pile and spilled off the edge. He caught it in one hand. The silky texture and sweet color detoured his thoughts.

No. He locked the image away. They needed to talk. He shoved the filmy fabric in his pocket.

"Last night. Beth's wedding. Our kiss?" His tongue stumbled as he said it. He'd like to get through this talking stuff, so they could move on to the doing part.

Daphne's eyes tightened slightly, then she smiled, but it looked more like a grimace. "Beth's little joke. Yeah, that was funny, wasn't it? What was she thinking?" She forced a laugh. "I wish I'd thought of something else to do with the thongs. None of the figures have outstretched hands, so all I can do is drape them over their heads."

"Daphne." Noah crossed the room and stood next to her. "That kiss told me something about us."

"That we're meant to be friends?" Her voice wavered. She stared blankly through the archway at the grinning Jeff

Gordon. Wrinkling her nose, she strode over to him and snatched the thong off his head.

"Is that what it told you?" Noah asked, following her.

She fidgeted with the cardboard man, testing the placement of the lipstick print thong on his figure. She spun away from him and headed for the kitchen. "I need scissors and tape."

Returning a few moments later, she snipped the elastic bands of the underwear and taped the remaining piece below the figure's waist. "What do you think?" she asked, as she tore a piece of tape off the dispenser.

"I don't think that's Jeff's color."

Daphne shook her head. "It blends into his suit." She relieved Jeff of the thong and headed for the kitchen again. Grabbing a fistful of silk from the table, she returned to the living room and tested the colors against the figure, barely sparing Noah a glance.

"The leopard print?" She grimaced and pressed fingertips against her eyes. "Why is this so hard? Maybe I have something in the car."

"Do you really think we can only be friends?" Noah asked quietly.

"Of course." Her voice quavered.

Noah reached for her arm and pulled her to him. He tilted her face toward his. What he saw wrenched his gut. Her tear-filled eyes refused to look up at him. He never wanted to see sadness in her eyes again. He was supposed to fix that. *Now.* "Then why are you crying?"

She brushed her hand across her eyes. "I'm not. My eyes are just watering. There must be smoke on your shirt. Did you wear it to a fire?"

"It's clean." He tugged her over to the sofa and they sat down. He wanted to crush her body next to his. Erase any vestige of tears. "Daphne, that kiss told me that we are meant to be together. You are the one for me." His tongue felt thick and unmanageable as he spoke the words. He thought they would come more easily after rehearsing them a hundred times in his head.

"It told you all that? Are you sure it wasn't the champagne?" Her voice cracked.

"We're perfect for each other, can't you see?"

"It wouldn't be fair." The tears flowed down her cheeks now.

"Why not?" *Couldn't she consider him for more than a millisecond?* He was tempted to grab her shoulders and shake her. Or kiss her senseless. *Wasn't he good enough for her to even consider?*

She smeared the tears across her cheek with the back of her hand. "What about the problem you have to fix? Isn't there someone else?"

Aaron didn't need to be fixed. Neutered, yes, and that was the least of what he deserved. He offered himself to her as himself, not as a replacement for Aaron. Daphne needed someone special, and he wanted to be that person.

"There's no one else, Daphne. There's only you. It's always been you." He brushed a loose strand of hair away from her cheek.

"So *I'm* the problem you have to fix?" A fresh cascade of tears traveled down her cheeks. She sprang from the couch and jabbed her finger into her chest. "What's wrong with me?"

*Oops.* Jeff Gordon grinned at him over her shoulder. *You stepped in it now,* he seemed to be saying. Then he remembered the leprechauns and saying he had to fix something before he could date anyone.

"No." He took a deep breath and let it out slowly. He held his hands out to her, wanting her to grasp them and say she understood what he wanted to say, that she knew what his heart was saying even though his tongue could not. *Couldn't she see that he loved her?* "Daphne, I want to date you."

"It wouldn't be right." She pressed her face into her palms and shook her head. Her ponytail brushed across her neck.

"Why not?" He ached to pull her hands away from her face and cradle her in his arms. Somehow, he thought, that would make his words come out right.

She smeared the tears across her face. The look of pain there broke his heart. "You're not Aaron."

## Chapter Nineteen

Daphne swung the loaded garbage bag over her shoulder and headed for the curb. The bag was stretching because she'd overstuffed it again, but she didn't want to pay the fee for an extra bag.

She couldn't believe Noah had shown up at Beth's. And then she'd blurted it out. *That he wasn't Aaron.* The look on his face told her he didn't understand.

Luckily for her, he'd turned on his heel and left, not giving her a chance to explain. She didn't think she'd be able to anyway.

The plastic gave way just as a blue SUV pulled into her driveway. Daphne's feet were covered with apple cores, wadded paper, and Aaron's stinky clothes. A run through the washer hadn't lessened their stench, and she wasn't calling him to come get them.

"Daphne Morrow?" A woman in a black suit and white blouse stepped out of the SUV. Dark sunglasses covered her eyes, and her blond hair was twisted in a tight French knot. Not a hair escaped in the summer humidity. Daphne wondered how much hairspray that required.

"What can I do for you?" Daphne asked, trying to push a blacked banana peel back into the bag with a wad of paper.

"Detective Widmore, Carterville PD. Could we talk for a few

minutes?" She flipped open a black leather wallet and flashed her badge as she walked across the sidewalk. "I have some questions about the Willows fire."

"I'm not sure how I can help. The paper said it was arson. What would I know about that?" Daphne gave up with the paper and bent down to shove the garbage back in the bag.

"The papers never get anything right." She pushed her sunglasses on top of her head and slipped her wallet into her shoulder bag. "Bag break?"

"Yeah. I overloaded it, trying to save money." Daphne grabbed Aaron's shirt and stuffed it in with the banana peels.

"That looks like a nice shirt."

"It was. In the nineties."

"I just cleaned out my closet. I had shorts from high school in there. Like those were ever going to fit again." She brushed her hand across her hip. "Took a whole pile of stuff to Goodwill," she said, nudging Aaron's shorts with the toe of her heeled boots. "These look like men's shorts. They yours too?"

*Damn.* Daphne had hoped she wouldn't notice that. She didn't want anyone to know she'd given into Aaron's pleading and allowed him into her house. She reached for the shorts to stuff them into the torn bag.

The detective tugged them away with her heel. The shorts spread out. "I would guess not."

Daphne sighed. "Ex-boyfriend's." At least she could say "ex." She wasn't entirely lying. "They still smell like him. I tried washing them, but the smell just wouldn't come out."

The detective bent and took a whiff. She whipped her head away. "Wow, that's nasty. Is that from the garbage?"

"Unfortunately, no."

"No wonder you dumped him." The detective shook her head.

Daphne grabbed the shorts and stuffed them in the bag. After adjusting the torn bag, she said, "I'm going to need another bag. Would you like to come inside?"

Detective Widmore nodded and gestured for Daphne to precede her. As the detective stepped through the doorway, she scanned the room.

She probably didn't miss a detail, from the torn pile of lime green fabric on the floor to the stacks of photographs and albums piled around the coffee table, Daphne thought. Thank goodness she'd washed the sheets Aaron had almost slept in and put them away. If the detective was so interested in his shorts, what would she think about sheets? Daphne thought, as she washed her hands.

"Have you been out to the Willows recently?" the detective asked, scanning the books stacked on Daphne's desk.

"No. Not since high school. How badly was it burned?" Daphne searched a kitchen cupboard for the box of garbage bags.

"It won't be called the Willows anymore. You went to Carterville High School, correct?" The detective stopped at a framed picture on the bookshelf. Daphne, sandwiched between her grinning parents, clutching a bouquet of roses and wearing a tiara. It was one of the few pictures of homecoming that didn't include Aaron.

"Class of nineteen ninety-eight."

The detective took the frame off the shelf and looked at the picture. "Homecoming queen?"

"Yeah. I've still got the tiara and sash around here somewhere. The school reuses the faux ermine cape."

"So you hold onto memories?"

"The good ones. I've been trying to sort out the bad ones." Daphne leaned against the counter separating the kitchen from the living room.

"Would this be one of the bad ones?" The detective pulled a photograph out of her shoulder bag.

Daphne walked around the coffee table to look at it and winced. It hurt to see her youthful joy and Aaron's wide grin. "I gave my last copy of that to my friend Noah."

"Last copy? What about the others?"

"Others?" Daphne shrugged. "Threw them away a few weeks ago."

"You look pretty happy in the picture. I must say you're quite photogenic. Why would you want to get rid of it?"

"Old boyfriend." Daphne tapped her finger against Aaron's grin.

"When'd you break up?"

"Every day for the last two years." Daphne sighed. Surely the detective had better things to do than talk about Daphne's old boyfriends. It certainly was a topic she had no wish to re-hash with a perfect stranger. The turmoil of the last few days, and this craziness with Noah, and Aaron showing up on her doorstep was wearing her down. "What does this have to do with the fire?"

"So you're just getting rid of the reminders?"

"It's been rough." She pushed the strands of hair escaping from her ponytail behind her ear.

"So rough you'd burn any reminders of him?"

"Burn?" Daphne shook her head. Then she understood. "I cut Aaron's head out of all the pictures and glued them to some ceramic donkeys I found at Goodwill. Then I smashed each one with a hammer. Are you asking if I burned the Willows?"

The detective raised an eyebrow.

"But you've been near a fire recently."

Daphne wracked her brain. *A fire? A campfire? A bonfire?* "Only the candles at my friend's wedding."

"The clothes in your garbage. They reek of smoke and al-cohol. You weren't wearing them when you burned these pic-tures out at the Willows?" The detective removed a scorched picture encased in plastic from her shoulder bag. She held it up and Daphne recognized enough of the picture to know it was a copy of the one she'd given Noah.

"Those aren't my clothes," Daphne said quietly, rubbing her hand over her face.

"I can make this easier for you. If you say the fire was an accident, we won't press charges. However, if we have to draw the investigation out, we'll be forced to ask for the maximum." The detective smiled as if she liked that idea.

"They're Aaron's."

"I thought you said you and Aaron broke up. What are his clothes doing in your garbage? Surely you haven't saved them, since you broke up over a year ago?"

"How'd you know that?"

"I know I wouldn't keep clothes that smelled that bad for very long." The detective arched her eyebrow.

Daphne sighed. "He stopped here a week ago. He wanted to crash on the couch."

The detective nodded as if she suspected that wasn't all Aaron wanted.

"I threw him out."

"Without his clothes?" The detective raised her eyebrow again.

*Yeah, I wouldn't believe that either,* Daphne thought.

"He had to leave quickly." Daphne hid a smile at the pink sweatpants. She waved to the garbage. "I tried to wash those, but the smell didn't come out and I wasn't going out of my way to give them back to him."

"What day was this?"

"Saturday night."

"The same day as the fire. Have you seen him since?" The detective pulled out a notebook and a pen.

The fleeting image of the red car after Noah dropped her off sped through Daphne's mind. She shook her head. "He said he was leaving town."

"Would he have a reason to burn his copy?" The detective flapped the picture.

"I told him to stop calling me the day before. That we were never going to get back together no matter how much he'd changed. I don't know what he would do with mementos of our relationship."

"Yet you let him stay over 'on the couch' within forty-eight hours?"

"I kicked him out after forty-five minutes. He knows what buttons to push. I couldn't listen to his mother complain about how I treated him again."

"Okay. Do you have any current contact information for him?"

Daphne shook her head. "He always called me, usually from a different cell phone. I think I have the most recent number on my caller ID." She went to the phone and scrolled back through the incoming numbers. "It's still here."

"I'll need a list of your whereabouts and anyone who can confirm them as well."

"Okay." Daphne grabbed a notepad from beside the phone. As she was writing, she asked, "Who gave you the picture?"

"Noah dropped it off at the station. He recognized the background. You know Noah, right? He's the cute one in the picture."

Daphne stopped writing. *Noah?* "When was this?"

"Friday morning. He stopped by the department with the picture. Told me all about your group of friends." Detective Widmore walked around the couch and watched over Daphne's shoulder as she wrote. "I'm surprised you don't have any pictures of him around. But some people don't appreciate what they've got."

*The whole weekend? He went the whole weekend without telling her the detective wanted to talk to her?*

*They spent how long in her car?* she fumed. And yesterday morning at Beth and Jake's. Her blood was getting hot.

He had to know Detective Widmore wanted to question her. He had to know. He gave the detective her name. And her address. *What else did he tell the detective?* The detective who obviously had a thing for him. What did she sweet-talk out of him?

*Why hadn't he warned Daphne? Did Noah suspect she set the fire? How could he?* He knew her better than that. Especially if he claimed they were meant for each other. Friends don't hide things like that from each other.

They couldn't date. Now they weren't friends. Could they salvage anything?

## Chapter Twenty

Daphne paced up and down Noah's driveway. The rain had washed out a channel in the gravel. She measured her steps to skip it on each pass. She had no idea when he'd return, but she was willing to let her anger fester until then. He deserved an earful.

*How could he turn the picture in to the detective without telling her?* He could have told her it matched the evidence, which Widmore made it obvious he knew. He could have asked her about it first. Given her a heads-up the detective might be asking questions. But no, he let the detective blindside her and back her into a corner.

She tried his cell phone a dozen times before storming over here. But he hadn't answered. *Did he suspect she started the fire and wanted to keep his distance? Was this revenge for keeping him at arm's length?*

She ground her teeth. No matter what their personal issues were, he had no right to pin the fire on her.

The anger and frustration whirled around in her head. A little voice whispered with too much logic that this wasn't the Noah she knew or the motives she could attribute to him, but she shoved it away. She didn't want to think logically right now. She kicked at the washout and sat on his front steps.

By the time Noah arrived home, Daphne's behind ached

from sitting on the cement stair, but she sprang up as he got out of his truck.

"You are such a jerk!"

Noah glanced at her and shut the door of his truck. He started toward the house.

"Well, hello to you too." He rubbed his hand across his face. "What brings you by?"

Daphne crossed her arms over her chest and blocked his path to the house.

"As if you don't know." She refused to let her eyes drop below the smear of soot around his collarbone. He'd ditched his shirt somewhere. She didn't need the sight of his tanned pectoral muscles and abdomen distracting her. Her eyes drifted downward and she jerked them up. *Where was his shirt?*

Noah backed against the truck. He rubbed his hand through his hair and glanced at his belt. The message light on his cell phone flashed frenetically. "You called?"

Daphne just stared at him.

He pushed himself off the truck and stepped around her. "A gas tank exploded in front of me." He headed for the house. "I can only handle one fire at a time."

"We're not finished here!" she shouted. She chased after him and grabbed for him to stop. If he'd been wearing a shirt, she would have caught that. Instead her hand slid down his back and caught the waistband of his shorts. Noah spun around and Daphne's fingers tangled between his belt and his belt loop. She came chest to chest with him with her arm around his waist.

Scents of smoke and sweat assailed her nose, but the overwhelming feeling was heat. Heat, as if they were standing too close to a bonfire. Daphne slowly raised her gaze from the sunbleached hairs on his chest to the barely perceptible cleft in his chin to his lips. Her breath hitched.

She wanted to feel his lips on hers again, and not in the chaste manner from Beth's wedding. She leaned toward him close enough to feel his breath on her cheeks. Her eyes slid closed and she succumbed to the headiness.

Noah's fingertips grazed the outside of her ear and tickled across her earlobe and her cheek. He cradled her chin between his thumb and forefinger and rubbed his thumb across her lower lip. Her tongue stretched to chase his movement, but she caught herself and her eyes sprung open. She tried to pull away, to untangle her fingers from his belt, but he caught her arm. His other hand cradled the back of her neck and urged her closer to him.

He pressed his lips to hers and growled, as Daphne accepted him and invited him further. A tiny thought niggled in the back of her mind that this was exactly the situation she'd wanted to avoid, but she couldn't wrangle enough resistance. In fact, she couldn't remember why she'd wanted to resist. His hand slid around her hips and pulled her body against his own. The very idea of struggling against this wonderful feeling fled. She angled her face and snaked her free arm around his neck. He groaned deep in his throat as Daphne dragged her nails through the short hair at the back of his head. Something about this wasn't right, but she didn't want to care.

But then she had a reminder.

Tires crunched against the gravel of his driveway and a car door slammed.

She pushed hard against Noah's chest and shoved him away from her.

Cool air rushed between them as Daphne stumbled back. Noah's chest heaved and Daphne yanked her gaze away from his sculpted muscles. Where her gaze landed wasn't much better. His eyes held fiery seduction. His jaw moved calculatingly, as if he were scheming to throw her over his shoulder and . . . He jerked his gaze toward the end of the driveway and his expression changed to steel. Daphne swiveled to see what had brought about the change.

"Aaron!" Noah and Daphne both exclaimed.

*What was Aaron doing here?* They'd agreed he was out of her life forever. *And what would he say?* If he mentioned he'd almost stayed at her house, she'd have to hurt him. Smashing donkey figurines with his face glued to them wouldn't relieve her anger this time.

Aaron strode down the driveway, leaving his cherry-red Camaro idling. His auburn curls brushed the collar of his polo shirt. He wore pleated khaki shorts and boat shoes. To Daphne, he looked thinner and more haggard than ten days ago.

"That's my name," he called, as he swaggered down the driveway. "Don't wear it out."

"I didn't know you were back in town." Noah moved so he stood slightly in front of Daphne. His body and presence provided a physical wall between her and Aaron. She wasn't sure who he was protecting from whom. He looked like he wanted to drop-kick Aaron to the other side of town. If that was the case, he'd have to get in line. She wanted to give both men a piece of her mind.

She stepped to the side so she had a clear view of Aaron.

"I can see that." He stepped away from Noah, moving closer to Daphne. "Moving in on my girl while my back's turned?" He said it to Noah, but his eyes studied Daphne.

"I'm not your girl, Aaron." Aaron never changed. No matter how many times she told him they weren't getting back together, he just didn't seem to get it. It was like he thought they would always be together no matter what he did. It had hurt when he dumped her, but she didn't miss his possessiveness.

"Right, my *woman*. Gotta be PC." He laughed as if the idea

was ridiculous. "You're looking"—he looked her up and down—"sooty. I really interrupted something."

He smeared a finger along the side of her face. She swatted his hand away and rubbed her cheek. Black dust marred her palm. Remembering how it got there made her heart pound. *How much had Aaron seen?*

Noah crossed his arms over his bare chest and stared at Aaron like a superhero daring his archenemy to make a bad move. *What did Noah think he was going to do?* She'd never seen him behave like this. He'd usually allow Aaron's snide comments to roll off his back.

"Yeah, I'm here on business, making some contacts, networking, you know, that kind of thing." Aaron stepped back and looked at his car at the end of the driveway. "Sweet ride, isn't it?"

"It's nice, Aaron. What do you want?" Noah asked.

Daphne wanted Aaron to get the heck out of Noah's driveway. She had a few things she wanted to get off her chest, but she didn't want an audience.

"I was on my way to Daphne's and I saw her car here," Aaron said, looking at Daphne. His voice sounded contrite. "I was hoping we could talk." His eyes sought hers like he was trying to send a message with them.

But she didn't tune into his wavelength anymore. She turned her head, purposefully ignoring his look.

"There's nothing left to talk about. I told you that the last time."

Aaron shifted his weight from foot to foot. He leaned toward her, putting Noah slightly behind his shoulder. His voice barely above a whisper, he said, "I've changed, Daphne. But I need some help."

"I can't go back there, Aaron." Her voice cracked. "I can't."

"That what the Magic Eight Ball said?"

Daphne flinched. He'd won the toy for her on one of their first dates. She'd kept it as a reminder that you couldn't depend on anything to turn out as you expected. The Eight Ball was only right when she least wanted it to be. It reminded her of all the things she wanted to avoid in her next relationship.

Aaron snorted. "I knew you still had it."

Noah moved between them. "You dumped her, Aaron. Leave her alone."

Daphne's jaw dropped open. If he was intending to defend her, he was doing a bang-up job. *Give the knife a good twist, Noah,* she thought.

"So you're fighting her battles for her now?" He snorted. "That how the wind blows? She's a good kisser, isn't she?"

Noah's chest expanded and he opened and closed his fists.

"Get off my property," Noah said, his voice low and menacing. "And leave Daphne alone."

Daphne had never heard that tone from Noah, and she didn't like it. *What gave him the right to defend her? Didn't he think she could fight her own battles?* She had dealt with Aaron many times.

Aaron smirked and tilted his head toward Daphne. "Do you think he would actually throw a punch over you? I'll just have to show Noah here how to get his butt kicked." He took his sunglasses off and hooked them on his shirt collar.

Noah flexed his hands. "The only rear end needing a boot print is yours. Daphne, you might want to stand back." He gently moved her away.

She threw his hands off her shoulder. "Do not push me around," she hissed. Aaron mumbled something about ending up in pink sweatpants, but she had ceased to care what he thought.

Daphne couldn't believe the scene unfolding in front of her. *Aaron and Noah weren't really coming to blows?* But they both seemed angry enough. Aaron was shaking his head with his usual swagger, and she could almost see the steam pouring out of Noah's ears. *What was the deal?* Whatever it was, she was taking Noah's advice. Before she stepped in the middle and punched them both. Heaven knows they both needed some sense knocked into them, but she wasn't going to sink to their level.

She pulled her keys from her pocket and headed for her car.

"Daphne, wait! I need to talk to you!" Aaron wailed.

She yanked open her door and lowered herself into the driver's seat.

"Daphne!" Noah called, as she wrenched the seatbelt across her lap. *Sure, now he wanted to talk to her.* Jamming her key into the ignition, she pulled her door shut. The engine roared to life and she wanted to scream along with it.

*Men.* The one she wanted to talk to wouldn't answer his phone and the one she didn't wouldn't leave her alone. Now they were squaring off, but she wasn't even sure what they were fighting about. They both wanted something from her, but neither one was going to get it. If they were trying to prove to her which one was more of a man—well, the answer to that question was obvious. They just needed to figure it out.

"You're both Neanderthals!" She jammed on the gas and the tires spun on the gravel. She stomped harder and the tires caught, rocketing her around the still-idling Camaro and down the street.

## Chapter Twenty-one

But what did Noah say then?"

Daphne pressed her ear to the phone, trying to separate Beth's voice from the airport loudspeaker announcing arrivals and departures on Beth's side of the connection. Daphne pulled the curtain aside and peeked out her window at her driveway.

"He didn't say anything. I left." Daphne pulled on the neckline of the one-shoulder white T-shirt Peggy insisted she and the other bridesmaids wear for her bachelorette party. *Bridesmaid* was spelled across her chest in silver sequins. The top was sure to become transparent should a smidgen of moisture come within twenty feet. Number four on Peggy's itinerary was the bar known for dousing its guests with the sprinkler system whenever the bartender received a generous tip. Daphne doubted she'd return home with a dry T-shirt.

"Oh crap. They're here."

The camouflage stretch Hummer came to a stop at the curb, and Peggy was standing through the open sunroof wearing her own strapless version of Daphne's shirt and a tiara with *bride* spelled out in rhinestones.

"Thanks for letting me know you made it home. We thought you'd be home a couple of days ago. Must have been nice to have a few extra days on your honeymoon." Daphne half-waved to Peggy through the window.

"Jake's boss gave us the perfect wedding gift—a few extra days off. We'll have to get together for coffee tomorrow. I want to hear everything."

"Okay. Peggy's yelling at me. I better go."

"Hey, Jake wants to know if you did anything to our house."

"What? I can't hear you. The connection." Daphne thumbed the end button on her phone and peeked out the window. She wasn't sure if she was up for this, but Peggy was her only female cousin, and she'd have to make the best of it. She grabbed a jacket, just in case, and shoved her wallet and keys in the pocket of her jeans.

Daphne pulled her front door shut and made her way down the sidewalk to the waiting limo. Unfortunately, she had no excuse but to climb into the camouflaged monstrosity and endure whatever tortures Peggy had planned for the evening.

Peggy ducked through the sunroof. A moment later, she popped through the door and rushed toward Daphne.

"Are you ready for a wild and crazy night?" she squealed, throwing her arms around Daphne.

"As ready as I'll ever be," Daphne said, trying to avoid getting scratched in the face by Peggy's tiara as she jumped up and down.

"This is going to be so much fun." Peggy grabbed her hand and dragged her into the limo.

Daphne climbed in and found a seat among the similarly attired bridesmaids. She took a bubbling glass of champagne and downed half of it before Peggy jammed a tiara on her head.

"I've got one for everyone."

The other women laughed and carefully adjusted their own tiaras. Daphne wondered how soon she could safely break hers. The plastic was already digging into her scalp.

She untangled the crown from her hair and bent the comb ends of the circlet until they snapped off. Shoving the combs between the seats, she replaced the tiara on her head. *Much better.* She could probably stand to wear it through the entire first stop of the party.

One of the other bridesmaids saw her and whipped her own tiara off and did the same thing. Daphne gave her a thumbs-up. She glanced around the interior of the limo at the other brides-maids, laughing and trying to keep their champagne flutes from sloshing as the limo turned down a gravel road. Peggy fum-bled with the handle of the mini bar and pulled out a fifth of schnapps.

"Minty shots for everyone." She poured a shot for herself and upended it down her throat. She passed the bottle and the shot glass to the next bridesmaid, who tentatively poured, then downed her own shot.

The bottle quickly made its way to Daphne, who pretended to pour and drink before passing the schnapps on. She didn't do well when she mixed her alcohols.

"Hey, I saw that," the bridesmaid who'd broken her tiara whispered to Daphne.

"I saw you too." Daphne said, as the other bridesmaid passed the bottle along. "But I won't tell."

"Someone's got to stay sane around her." She tugged her bridesmaid T-shirt, pulling the side that dipped under her arm up. "You don't remember me, do you?"

Daphne studied her a moment. "Merry? Dustin's little sister?"

Merry nodded. Daphne gave her a quick hug. "I haven't seen you since your graduation."

"I've been teaching English in Thailand for the last two years. I'm back for the summer, so I can participate in all the festivities." She nodded to Peggy, who was pulling little bags out of a basket and passing them around the group. The bags were red and blue cellophane with silver ribbons tying them closed.

"Oh no, what's this?" Daphne asked, reluctantly accepting a bag from the bridesmaid on her right.

Merry tore off the silver ribbon and reached into the bag. She removed a small cylindrical container and flipped it over to read the label. "Body glitter?"

"Isn't it great?" Peggy squealed. She untwisted the lid and smeared a generous dab across her chest.

"So she's still crazy?" Merry murmured to Daphne.

"As if the T-shirts didn't make that clear." She dumped her bag into her lap. "At least its only body glitter and lipstick. Rather tame for Peggy, I'd say."

Merry snorted. "Until you read the name of the color: Red Light District."

"Probably where she bought it."

Peggy made lip-smacking sounds as she looked into her compact mirror. The hooker red glowed on her lips. The other bridesmaids followed Peggy's example and smeared their lips. Daphne and Merry grimaced at each other.

"We should probably do one of them."

"I vote for body glitter," Merry said. "I don't want to look like a vampire fresh from a feeding."

Daphne nodded and shoved the lipstick between the seats with her tiara combs.

"First stop. Belly Up!" Peggy shouted. She pushed the limo door open and swayed on the step outside, but managed to keep her balance as she climbed down. Daphne and Merry followed the rest of the party across the gravel parking lot.

"Belly Up? That's the name of the place?" Merry asked when they arrived at the door. A hand-painted sign over the door showed a man resting his distended gut on the bar.

"Classy, huh?" Daphne held the door and the rest of the group trooped in.

They crowded into a large circular booth. The smoky haze was broken only by the neon lights circling the mirrored beer advertisements and the dancing figures wearing cowboy hats and sleeveless white T-shirts.

Daphne gladly scooted to the center of the booth, away from the unshaven men propositioning other members of her party for dances. Merry joined her, nursing a diet soda and trying to catch up on all the happenings in Carterville since she'd left.

When the nicest-looking man Daphne'd seen since entering the bar—his shirt had buttons and he appeared to have showered in the last twenty-four hours—asked her to dance, Daphne couldn't refuse. Especially since Peggy answered for her and yanked her out of the booth.

Daphne grimaced in what she hoped looked like a half-smile and took the man's hand. He tugged her onto the dance floor. They started to dance, but gliding was nearly impossible when her sandals and his cowboy boots stuck to the floor.

"Must have spilled some drinks here earlier," Daphne said, as her sandals made a telltale *squelch-squerch* from the sticky residue.

"Nah. It's always like that. My name's Tucker," the man said, as he placed his hand on her waist and took her other hand in his own. They hopped around to the country music and Daphne felt some of her funk fading away. Merry waved as she stepped on the dance floor with a young man who barely looked old enough to legally imbibe alcohol, but then Merry was a couple of years younger than Daphne.

"You named after that news commentator?" she asked.

"What?"

Daphne shook her head. "Never mind."

"Bridesmaid, huh? When's the wedding?"

"How'd you figure that one out?" Daphne asked sarcastically while navigating a turn.

"It was the first thing that caught my eye." He grinned, showing a full set of teeth.

Daphne glanced down at her shirt. He could read. It could be worse. She could be dancing with Aaron. Hopefully, he'd left town for good. She didn't want to see his face again anytime soon.

She'd still like to give Noah a chunk of her mind. First the thing with Detective Widmore. Then the face-off with Aaron.

She'd never seen Noah anything but calm and cool. Even when her "pool" put a square-foot hole in the back of his truck where the rust gave way under the weight of the water. He'd just shrugged and said, "Oh, well." Then he'd grinned.

But lately, she was seeing another side of him. One that had strong buried passions. Like their kiss. She'd never imagined anything could ignite between them like that fire. Her body warmed just remembering. She didn't think she could reconcile the two Noahs into anything she could be friends with.

She moved to put a few more inches between her body and Tucker's. The sequins on her T-shirt winked through the cigarette smoke.

"Wedding's in two weeks. My cousin's having her final fling." She glanced back at the table where Peggy was gyrating on the table with moves Daphne had only seen in the movie *Striptease*. The bouncer was pushing his way through the crowd toward her.

"I guess even this place has standards," Daphne mumbled. She attempted to untangle herself from Tucker. "I should probably help her out."

"Hold on a sec." He fished an ink pen from his pants pocket and jotted some numbers on her wrist. "Call me sometime."

"Whatever," Daphne called, as she hurried away from the dance floor. She arrived at the table in time to see Peggy lifted down by the bouncer.

"He says we gotta go," she whined. "Can you believe that?"

"I sure can," Daphne mumbled, rounding up the other women and heading back to their monster chariot. Merry grabbed a couple of stragglers and steered them toward the door.

"Where you going?" Tucker asked as Daphne half-carried, half-dragged Peggy out the door.

"I hope it's home," Daphne mumbled. She'd had enough of this crazy bachelorette party, and Peggy was too drunk to walk steadily. Daphne assumed there'd be no problem getting Peggy to agree.

That's the thing about assumptions.

"We're going to karaoke!" Peggy slurred, as Tucker held the door open for them.

Daphne rolled her eyes and shoved Peggy toward the limo.

"Maybe I'll see you there," Tucker called, pointing his finger at her and making a clicking sound.

*Over my dead body,* Daphne thought. She sank into one of the overstuffed seats, wishing only for her bed. Merry sat across from her, pressing her palms against her temples as if her head would explode if she let go.

Dancing with Tucker hadn't done anything to erase Noah from her mind, to remove his scent from her senses or the memory of his lips on hers.

Daphne assumed the limo driver would drop them off one by one, and she could retreat to a warm bath and then perhaps the last two days would disappear into her distant memory. Unfortunately, the limo stopped in front of the only karaoke place in town. The rest of the girls piled out. Daphne wondered if she could stay in the vehicle, but Peggy grabbed her wrist and dragged her out of the limo and into the smoky pizza joint. The pizza place was packed, with barely a table available. A group of men fueled by liquid courage belted out "Ring of Fire." They mumbled through the verses and yelled the chorus.

Peggy ordered the servers to push a couple of tables together in front of the stage. Daphne and the other women sat down as the servers arranged paper place mats, napkin-rolled plastic silverware, and sweating water glasses around the table. Daphne gulped her water gratefully, trying to wash away the lingering effects of her previous stop.

The singing trio finished to shouts and cheers from the crowd. They descended the steps clumsily and wandered back to their table.

"What should we sing?" Peggy asked, snatching the song list from the center of the table. Daphne glanced at the list over Peggy's shoulder and winced when she saw "Wannabe" by the Spice Girls, a song she knew was one of Peggy's favorites.

"How about 'Girls Just Wanna Have Fun'?" Daphne suggested, pointing to the opposite page, well away from the Spice Girls' hit. "We can all do that one."

"Okay." Peggy hopped from her seat and trotted up to the sign-up station.

Daphne ordered a plain Coke and a couple of pizzas for the whole table.

"She was going to pick the Spice Girls one, wasn't she?" Merry asked. When Daphne nodded, she said, "Thank you."

"We're on next after this group," Peggy said, when she returned. Several of the other women squealed in excitement. Daphne just nodded. They would get the humiliation over quickly.

Peggy grabbed her arm and started dragging her toward the stage.

"Come on. It's our turn!" Penny giggled. Daphne sighed and pushed herself up from the table. Her feet did not move of their own volition, but the rest of the group carried her along.

The DJ handed them mics and they all crowded around the screen, waiting for the words to pop up. Daphne glanced at the crowded dining room and saw Noah, Dustin, and several other men crowded around a table in the rear. The music started and the crowd catcalled. Daphne focused on the words as they changed color on the screen. She didn't think their singing was that good, but the audience whistled and several men stood, clapping and cheering.

Daphne glanced at the screen behind her and forgot the next words of the song. The video that went with the music portrayed several women in bikinis painting each other with finger paints. She turned back to the monitor with the words and saw Peggy singing and dancing as if she had a pole.

Daphne doubted the night could get any more embarrassing. She'd hoped to maintain at least an ounce of dignity when she'd seen Noah from the stage, but Peggy obviously wouldn't let that happen.

The song finally ended and the male half of the crowd cheered and howled.

Three men climbed the stairs to the stage and Daphne's heart dropped as soon as she saw Noah among them. Daphne avoided his gaze, instead concentrating on the handrail on her other side. She felt his fingers brush her arm, sending electricity shooting through her body. She hurried down the stairs, anxious to put space between them.

"What are you doing here?" Peggy shrieked above the murmur of the dining room. Daphne glanced over her shoulder. Peggy and Dustin were standing in the middle of the stairs. "You said your party would be gone by the time we got here. I can't have the fun I'm supposed to have at my bachelorette party if you're here watching."

"According to the schedule, you weren't supposed to arrive until seven-thirty," Dustin shouted. "It's only seven."

Peggy's jaw moved up and down, but she didn't say anything. Obviously she'd been thrown out of Belly Up earlier than she'd planned.

Daphne backpedaled up the stairs and caught Peggy's arm. "It's not so bad. Maybe they'll sing a romantic song for you."

Dustin looked at Noah, who was talking to the DJ. "I don't know what Noah is picking." He shrugged.

"Whatever they sing, just pretend it's a love song to you," Daphne said, dragging Peggy back to their table.

Sitting down at their table with Peggy, who was mostly mollified, Daphne sipped her Coke. It's a small town, she wouldn't be able to avoid Noah forever, but she had hoped for at least forty-eight hours. He and his friends circled around the microphone and he detached it from its stand.

He looked directly at her.

"This song is dedicated to a special woman out there. I wish things could be different." His gaze never left hers.

The DJ started the music and the first strains of "Jessie's Girl" flowed from the speakers. Daphne remembered watching the video with Noah and Aaron and some of their other friends in high school.

Daphne wanted to crawl under the table or run to the bathroom, anything to hide from his gaze. She knew if she did, it would tell him their conversation affected her more than she wanted him to believe. She tried to sip her Coke as calmly as she could. Studying the outdated sports schedule on the place mat in front of her, she counted the seconds until the song was over. Her ears picked out Noah's voice, even though the three men blended well together.

*Why couldn't it be different,* she asked herself as she drew circles on her place mat with the condensation from her glass. It just couldn't. It would ruin their friendship. If they even had one left. People just couldn't be friends again after they had dated. She couldn't date someone who thought she was an arsonist.

Besides, they worked together and saw each other almost every day during the school year. It'd be awkward for the whole school if it didn't work out. Long pauses during the coaches' meetings when someone said something wrong.

Other teachers sneaking glances at them, and e-mails flying around the building.

She'd been through it after Aaron dumped her, and she couldn't do it again.

Daphne hurried straight for the bathroom as the song finished. She didn't want Noah stopping to talk to her. What she needed to say to him should be said in private. She needed a few moments of peace and quiet before she could face the rest of the evening with Peggy.

Unfortunately, the bathrooms were single stall and a line had already formed for the "Gals." Daphne leaned against the wall and crossed her arms over her chest. She stared down at the floor, trying to ignore the excited chatter of the two women next to her.

"Hey, that was some singing," a familiar voice said way too close to her ear. "I liked the video."

Daphne looked up into Aaron's grinning face. He winked at her and leaned against the wall next to her, blocking her view of the dining room.

Her Magic Eight Ball was right. The evening had gone from humiliating to mortifying in a matter of seconds.

"It was something all right." She cast a furtive glance at the bathroom door, which remained obstinately closed.

He leaned closer. "Want to ditch the party and come home with me?" His lips brushed her ear. "I have some body paint."

Daphne managed to stop her gag reflex. She was about to tell him what she thought of that idea with a sharp elbow to the ribs, when one of the women on her other side stumbled and bumped Daphne into Aaron's chest. She tried to catch herself with the aforementioned elbow, but ended up mashed against his cotton shirt and choking on the scent of his cologne. In an attempt to steady her, he wrapped his arm around her and squashed her tighter against him.

"Were you in line for the men's room?" Noah asked, stepping around Aaron. "Oh." He cleared his throat. "Hi, Daphne."

Daphne extricated herself from Aaron's grasp. She pushed her bangs away from her face. "Hi, Noah." Her cheeks had to be sunburn red. Aaron slipped his arm over her shoulder.

Noah glanced from her to Aaron and back, a question in his eyes. He stared at her for a moment, and Daphne shrugged Aaron's arm off. He brushed his hand across her behind as he returned it to his side. Daphne jammed her heel down on his toe.

He cursed and hopped on his uninjured foot, cradling the injured one.

"Keep your hands to yourself," Daphne said, moving to the opposite side of the hallway and out of his reach.

The door to the "Guys" room opened and Aaron waved Noah between them.

Noah looked at Daphne and moved his lips as though he was going to say something, but shook his head and pushed open the bathroom door.

"I want my shoes back."

"Go and get them. They're on my back deck."

"You put them outside? They're four-hundred-dollar shoes!"

"They stunk to high heaven. You're lucky I didn't toss them with the rest of your clothes."

He shook his head. "It doesn't matter. You've got to help me, Daphne." Aaron stopped hopping and leaned toward her. "I think I'm in trouble."

"I don't have to do anything. Whatever your problems are, they're yours." Daphne shook her head. "I can't help you."

"I just need you to talk to the police. Tell them you saw me on Saturday."

"I already told them I saw you."

"Could you call them back and tell them it was a little earlier than you remembered?"

"How much earlier?" Daphne's eyes narrowed. He was a fool to think she'd lie for him, but she was curious to see where this was going.

"Saturday morning, maybe Friday night."

"Friday night? Like Friday night when the Willows fire was started? Did you have anything to do with that?"

"I might have. I don't remember." He scrubbed his hand through his hair. The dim light of the hallway deepened the shadows under his eyes.

Daphne slumped against the wall. "I can't lie for you. No one would believe me. I was at Miranda's wedding reception until shortly before you showed up."

Aaron mumbled a colorful curse.

"In fact, the police already know because they tried to pin the fire on me. They found your clothes."

"What?"

"Detective Widmore saw your shirt and shorts as I was taking them to the garbage. Turns out she recognized the smell of smoke on them."

Aaron's curses moved from colorful to obscene.

"You could turn yourself in. Explain what happened."

"How can I explain what I don't know? They're going to throw me in jail and it will be your fault."

"Because I wouldn't lie for you?"

"If you had taken me back, I wouldn't have burned your pictures."

"That's why you started the fire?" Daphne gasped. She wasn't sure what surprised her more: that he started the fire or that he was pretending to not remember doing it.

"It doesn't matter now. It's over." He mimicked her voice. He leaned toward her again and Daphne wished the hallway wasn't so narrow. The look on his face sent a cold stab of fear through her stomach, and she wanted to get away from him, but he blocked the hallway to the dining room. "I'm not going to jail because of you."

The bathroom door opened and Noah stepped out. "Excuse me," he mumbled as he ducked between them.

Daphne hooked her arm through his. "I'm not finished with you," she said.

Aaron stepped aside and Noah and Daphne exited the hallway. Daphne didn't dare a backward glance as she marched Noah through the dining room and out to the parking lot.

When they reached the lot, Noah shook her hand away.

"What is this all about, Daphne? Why did you want to get away from Aaron?" Noah threw his hands up in the air. "Man, I feel like an idiot."

"I'm not here with Aaron. In case you missed the whole group of us in Hooters' shirts and tiaras, I'm with Peggy's bachelorette party." Daphne removed her tiara and pushed her fingers through her hair. "Thanks for your help. I needed an extraction."

"An extraction? I thought you wanted Aaron." Noah sighed. He turned away from her.

"I don't." Daphne waved the tiara at him, tempted to fling it at his back.

Noah turned back to her. His eyes met hers. She could see the anger and hurt warring there.

"He had his hands all over you and you didn't look upset about it."

"The woman next to me bumped me into him. He kept me from hitting the floor."

"If that's all it was, why did you need an extraction?"

"Aaron keeps showing up. I didn't tell you, but he showed up at my house after Miranda's wedding. He wanted to get back together."

Noah closed his eyes and pressed his fingertips against his

forehead. "If that's what you want, why'd you use me to get away from him?"

"I don't want to be with Aaron." *Why would he ever think that?* He knew everything Aaron had put her through.

"You don't want Aaron. You don't want me because I'm not Aaron. What do you want?"

Daphne's jaw dropped open. Her mouth moved to form words, but she couldn't find the ones to express her disbelief at his comments. Why would he think she wanted Aaron? Why would she want Noah to be like Aaron—a narcissistic philanderer? She wanted Noah to be her friend. Just like he'd always been. The sexual tension bubbling between them had no place in their relationship.

"Yeah. That's what I thought." He turned back to the parking lot and walked into the darkness.

"You don't understand. I don't want to lose you as a friend." Her voice was quiet, but he still stopped.

"I can't just be friends anymore, Daphne. I can't bear having only part of you." His eyes were shaded from the lights of the parking lot, but they still pierced her heart.

She tried to edge the sharpness away. Tried to keep it from piercing deeper, but it kept sinking home. She couldn't take that step with Noah. It wasn't right for their relationship. But their old relationship was gone. She didn't think even an ounce of it could be salvaged.

She felt wetness on her cheeks and smeared the tears. Then drops hit her shoulder and hair. *Rain.*

Noah glanced at the sky and then back toward his truck. "See you around, Daphne." He strode away.

## Chapter Twenty-two

Noah slowed to a walk and fished his flashlight out of his shorts' pocket. Daphne wasn't home yet. He could take a peek at Aaron's shoes and get out of there. He had to know if Aaron started the fire. He was the only one it could be. He was the only one with a reason to burn the pictures. Noah had heard enough while he was in the bathroom to be suspicious. He thought about calling Detective Widmore, but figured there'd be issues with warrants even if the shoes were right outside.

Noah didn't like Aaron visiting Daphne, but there wasn't anything he could do about it. Daphne had made it quite plain her life was her business and he should keep out of it.

He made his way around the side of her house. He flicked on the flashlight as he stepped into the shadows away from the streetlights. The light cast a golden cone on the grass and he quickly found the stairs up to her deck.

Mounting the steps, he wondered why he was here. He'd planned to jog around the block and clear his head, but his flashlight winked at him before he left home. He'd shoved it in his pocket, refusing to acknowledge why he would take it along with him.

He swung the flashlight's beam around the deck. Daphne's lounge chairs were angled in perfect arrangement to catch the rays of the sun. Just off the mat outside the slider was a pair of men's leather shoes.

Something dark rolled in his stomach. Aaron hadn't been teasing her about his clothes. They were actually there. How did he leave his clothes here? Thoughts spun through Noah's head, but he pushed them aside. He didn't want to imagine it. It wasn't his business anymore.

Picking up one shoe, he flashed the light over it. Dirt and ash clung to it. Ash. So Aaron was the one.

"Freeze!" a female voice shouted from behind him.

Noah froze with the right shoe in his hand. A large flashlight from the yard blinded him. Noah dropped his flashlight and raised his hand to shield his eyes.

"Police!" a female voice yelled again. "Put your hands up." He heard someone climb the steps behind him.

Noah raised his arms slowly and turned his face to the side to avoid the bright lights. Had one of Daphne's neighbors seen him and called the police about a prowler?

The flashlight rounded the deck and mounted the stairs. The man carrying it grabbed the shoe from Noah's hand and pulled his arms down and behind his back.

"I'm Officer Hopkins and this is Officer Baldus," the female officer said, flashing her badge. They were dressed in dark T-shirts and jeans. Were they off-duty? She quickly frisked him. Luckily, Noah was only wearing shorts and a T-shirt, so it would have been pretty hard to hide a weapon anywhere.

"Aaron Banks, you are under arrest," Officer Hopkins said, as she encased Noah's wrists in handcuffs.

"I'm not Aaron," Noah said, trying to look over his shoulder. Something in the back of his mind laughed at Daphne's accusation coming out of his mouth. *No,* he wasn't Aaron and he was tired of being mistaken for him.

"Sure. That's what they all say." Officer Hopkins pulled her

Miranda Rights card out of her pocket and read it to Noah, shoving him toward the stairs.

"I'm not." He glanced back at Officer Baldus, who had retrieved the other shoe from beside the slider and was putting the pair into a paper bag. Noah knew a few of the officers on the Carterville police force, but didn't recognize either of these two. They must be rookies.

"We'll just see what your fingerprints say when we get to the station." Officer Hopkins guided him to the plain dark sedan parked across the street.

*Unmarked car? Had they been watching Daphne's house?*

Officer Hopkins yanked the rear door open and Noah climbed in the back seat. No use fighting this until they got to the station.

Officer Baldus secured the bag of shoes in the trunk, then climbed in the driver's seat. Officer Hopkins scooted into the shotgun seat and grabbed the handset for the radio.

Voices from dispatch cracked over the speaker, then she said, "Tell her we have him. We're on our way to the station."

Officer Baldus navigated the car through town. The police scanner squawked and one of the officers moved to turn down the volume. Noah heard something about "bringing her in," "disorderly conduct," and "a live one." He thought of Peggy, but if Daphne was with her, she'd stay out of any serious trouble. They pulled into the station a few minutes later.

The female officer opened Noah's door and pulled him out of the car, keeping her hand at his elbow until they reached the police and fire station. The other officer jerked the door open and officer Hopkins pushed him through. She walked him down a narrow hallway and then into the small office area used by the Carterville police force.

After handcuffing one of his hands to the chair, she slipped into the seat behind the desk and powered up the computer.

She drummed her fingers on the keyboard until the computer beeped it was ready.

"Name," she said.

"Noah Anderson Banks."

She scowled at him. "If you're going to be difficult, I'll add resisting arrest to your recommended charges."

"I swear that's my name."

She picked up a memo from the desk. "Aaron Banks. Description. Six feet. One hundred eighty pounds. Brown hair. Blue eyes." She cast him a sidelong glance. "One eighty? I'd say two hundred. Looks like you've been pumping some iron."

"Or I'm not Aaron," he tried to reason with her.

"Likely not. Address?"

"Just look up my driver's license. You can see the picture."

"Our database doesn't have pictures."

Noah rubbed the bridge of his nose. He should have stayed home. Drank the last two beers in his fridge and tumbled into bed. But no, he had to go for a jog.

The officer's fingers clicked on the keyboard. Then she read, "Noah Anderson Banks. Six one. One ninety-five. Brown hair. Blue eyes." She arched her eyebrow. "Not much different. Anyone else you want to claim to be?"

Noah shook his head. "My name is Noah. Aaron is my cousin. You're looking for him because you think he started the Willows fire."

"No. We're looking for *you* in regards to the Willows fire. Why else would you be trying to steal the evidence?"

Noah groaned. How could he prove who he was? No other officers were at the station. The dispatch operator would recognize him, but her office was at the county building. Maybe she'd recognize his voice over the radio.

"You could call—" he started, but was interrupted by Detective Widmore.

"Noah? What are you doing here?" she called from the

doorway. Her blonde hair was pulled back in a lazy ponytail. She wore a fitted cotton shirt, a beige skirt, and open-toed pumps. Why was she so dressed up this late at night?

He didn't care. Relief flooded through him. Finally someone who could get him out of this mess.

"They think I'm Aaron," he said, tilting his head to the two officers.

"He came looking for the shoes, just like you said he would," Officer Hopkins piped up. "We arrested him on her deck."

The detective's face slid into a cool mask. Noah wasn't sure what she was thinking and began to feel nervous again. The detective shook her head.

"No. This isn't him. Although I'm curious to know what you planned to do with the shoes, Noah."

Officer Hopkins scooted her chair away from the desk and unlocked Noah's handcuffs. He rubbed his wrists absently. "I just wanted to see if it was true."

"True? Do you have some other suspect you're not telling me about?" The detective placed her hands on her hips and looked down at him.

"No. I overheard a conversation earlier tonight and wanted confirmation." He didn't tell her he was looking for confirmation of more than just the fire.

Ellen glanced at the two rookies, who appeared to be waiting for instructions. "Go back out there and wait for him. You better hope he hasn't been and gone while you were on this little shenanigan." She dismissed the officers and turned to Noah. "I know he's going to show up there. Their relationship isn't as over as you think it is. Let's go to my office and we can discuss this conversation you overheard."

Noah stood and followed Ellen to her office. Once there, she closed the door and wandered behind her desk. She shuffled a couple of papers, then returned to the front and leaned against it. She gestured for Noah to sit in the chair in front of her.

Noah didn't feel comfortable sitting with her towering over him, so he walked to the window and leaned against the frame.

"I should thank you," he said after a moment. "Officer Hopkins wouldn't believe I wasn't Aaron."

"They're lied to all the time. So what did you overhear?" She reached behind her head and pulled the band from her ponytail. She ran her fingers through her hair and shook out the tangles.

Noah gave her the highlights of the conversation he'd overheard. She nodded every now and then, but didn't write anything down.

"That confirms Daphne's story," she said when he'd finished.

"And that Aaron started the fire," Noah added. "He practically admitted it."

The detective was silent. "We'll know more when we get the tests back on the shoes."

"They were definitely men's shoes," he insisted. "I told you it wasn't Daphne."

Ellen stood up and shook her head. "Why do you keep defending her? I doubt she'd do the same for you."

"We're friends." Then he pictured Daphne standing in the parking lot earlier this evening, and his words came back to him. "We used to be," he mumbled.

Ellen's features perked up. "Huh. Well, we'll get this all straightened out. Now about thanking me for dragging you away from the wolves out there." She gestured toward the main office. "I'll drive you home."

## Chapter Twenty-three

Daphne shivered as the rain spattered harder against her bare shoulder. She couldn't believe he'd just walked away. She stared at the parking lot exit where his taillights had disappeared.

She hugged her arms to her chest. All or nothing. He wouldn't accept anything in between.

If that was what he wanted, fine. She could do *nothing*. No problem.

A squeal that could only come from one set of vocal cords erupted behind her.

She just didn't think she could do *nothing* on Peggy's itinerary. She turned to greet the other bridesmaids pouring out of the bar.

"It's raining." Peggy laughed, holding her hands out to the sky. Raindrops splashed against her chest, revealing the black push-up bra she wore under her T-shirt. "So this is where you've been hiding." She hooked her arm through Daphne's and pulled her toward the waiting Hummer.

"Peggy," Daphne said in a low voice. "I'm not feeling well. Do you mind if I go home?"

Peggy stopped in her tracks and turned Daphne to face her. "Of course I mind. Daphne, this is my bachelorette party. You're my only cousin. You have to be here."

Daphne bit her lip. "Okay. One more stop. Then I'm going

home." She adjusted the tiara, steeling herself for another half hour.

Peggy gave her a quick hug. "After the next stop, you'll be ready to party all night. I promise." Daphne allowed Peggy to help her into the limo. She couldn't remember the next stop on Peggy's itinerary. Nothing came to mind. All she knew was that it wasn't the sprinkler place.

Daphne found a seat in the limo and accepted the glass of champagne Merry offered her. She took a small sip, then lowered the flute.

"Is everything okay?" Merry asked quietly, scooching into the seat next to her.

"Probably not, but I promised Peggy I'd go to the next stop." Daphne rubbed her temples.

"We'll call you a cab when we get there. I'll think of something to tell Peggy. In fact, once she gets inside, she probably won't even notice you're gone."

"I doubt that."

"She won't notice anything but what's on stage at Pipes." Merry sipped her own drink. "You'll be able to duck out."

When they arrived at Pipes, Peggy practically ran toward the door. Daphne, Merry, and the other bridesmaids followed at a more grown-up pace. Once inside, Daphne understood why Peggy would be distracted. Dancing on stage were four men in tuxedo pants and bow-ties. The oil on their skin glistened, highlighting well-sculpted muscles.

Peggy pushed through the crowd until she was right in front of the stage, waving her hands in the air.

"How'd you know about this place, but not Belly Up?" Daphne asked Merry.

"Dustin had a flier. I guess they alternate nights with male and female dancers. Peggy must have gotten her way for choosing the night for the parties." Merry glanced at the stage. "Let's get you a cab."

As they waited for the cab to arrive, they watched Peggy beg for dollar bills from each of the bridesmaids. At the end of the dance, she clapped wildly.

"Sorry to ditch you like this," Daphne said when her cab arrived.

"Not a problem. I still owe you for getting me through senior English. I'll see you at the next event." She drew finger quotes around *event* and waved Daphne off. Daphne gratefully climbed into the cab and leaned back in the seat as the driver pulled away.

The whole night had been one gigantic nightmare, and Daphne was only glad it was over.

Until an hour later, when the phone rang.

Daphne had no more than climbed in bed with her *Complete Jane Austen* and found a comfortable spot, when the phone started ringing. She considered ignoring it, but decided to check the caller ID anyway.

She padded into the living room and looked at the display. *Carterville Police.* Did the police find Aaron? If he was calling her to bail him out, she'd let him rot. It was more than he'd deserve.

Picking up the handset, she prepared herself to hear his voice begging her to help him out yet again.

Instead, Peggy screeched into the phone, "They took my tiara, Daphne! They took it!"

"What are you doing at the police station?" Daphne asked, flipping on a light and searching for a pen and paper.

"He wouldn't get close enough and I had a twenty, for goodness' sake. Then the police took my tiara."

"Peggy," Daphne asked, "what are you talking about?"

Her voice switched from whiny to angry. "I've been arrested, Daphne, and it's all your fault. Some cousin you are." She huffed at the end.

"Arrested? What happened?"

"Just get down here and get me out of jail. Oh, and bring your checkbook. The guard guy says you have to pay a hundred bucks or something." Peggy hung up before Daphne could ask any more questions.

Daphne quickly dressed in shorts and a T-shirt and pulled her hair back into a ponytail. She grabbed her keys off the end table and hurried out the door. She wasn't sure whether Peggy's bail would go up or down the longer she was in custody. Would the officials lower it to get rid of her or raise it because of her obnoxiousness?

Daphne wondered how she'd find Peggy, but all she had to do was follow the screeching when she entered the building. Peggy was handcuffed to a chair next to a paperwork-covered desk. The officer occupying the desk looked in worse shape than Peggy was. He was hunched over his keyboard, trying to ignore Peggy's rants about her tiara and her bachelorette party being ruined.

"I can't believe you left me," Peggy snapped, as soon as she spied Daphne in the doorway of the office. "This never would have happened if you had been there. People listen to you."

The officer stood and walked over to Daphne. "Are you here to bail her out?"

"Do I have to be?"

"I want you to be." The officer cringed as Peggy started to whine about the temperature of her coffee. He mumbled something about decaf and turned back to Daphne.

"What happened?" Daphne dug through her purse for her checkbook.

"She was at Pipes and started harassing one of the dancers. He says she climbed onstage and grabbed his butt." The officer's cheeks turned red.

Daphne couldn't keep her jaw from dropping. "You're kidding?"

"I wish I was. I haven't been able to get her side of things. All she'll talk about is that damn tiara." He glanced back at Peggy, who was checking her makeup in the surface of the stapler.

"It's all her fault, officer. She's my only cousin and my bridesmaid and she ditched my bachelorette party. What kind of friend does that?" Peggy called.

"A pretty good one if she's here to bail you out," he responded.

Peggy's eyes narrowed, but she kept her mouth shut.

"She can have the tiara back once she's out of custody. I'll get the paperwork for you to sign." He headed for his desk.

Daphne approached Peggy. "He said you assaulted one of the dancers?"

"Well, I didn't mean to. He makes it sound like I did it on purpose. I stumbled when I climbed onstage and grabbed the first thing I could to catch myself."

"You're not supposed to go onstage. Didn't you see the signs? 'Please appreciate the dancers with your eyes only.' "

Peggy rolled her eyes. "Then how are you supposed to stuff the dollar bills in their pants? I had a twenty for him. He was good." She nodded her head.

"Was anyone else climbing onstage?"

Peggy thought for a moment. "No, but no one else had a tiara or was the bride at their own bachelorette party that their favorite cousin ditched. I think that gives me special privileges."

"Obviously the dancer didn't agree." Daphne signed the paperwork the officer presented her and handed him a check for Peggy's bail.

He unlocked Peggy's handcuffs. "You're free to go. We'll contact you if the dancer decides to press charges."

Daphne grabbed Peggy's arm and ushered her to the hallway. Peggy pulled away and poured herself another cup of coffee before following Daphne.

"What were you thinking?" Peggy asked as soon as they left the office. "Leaving my party like that?"

Daphne sighed. Would it be worth explaining everything to Peggy? Probably not, but Peggy deserved an explanation, being her only cousin and all.

"I had a fight with Noah and it really upset me. I didn't want to be a downer for your party."

"What'd you fight about?" Peggy asked.

"I'd rather not talk about it here."

"Well, here is where we are going to talk about it. I'm not leaving until I get an explanation." Peggy planted her feet and thrust her fresh cup of coffee at Daphne. "You ruined my party."

Daphne glanced back at the office, wondering if the officer would arrest her for not removing the public disturbance quickly enough.

"This really isn't the time or place," Daphne said, but Peggy wouldn't budge. She tried another tack. "Come on. It's late."

"Miss! You forgot your tiara." The officer emerged from the office with the plastic crown in his hand.

"Oh, thank you." Peggy took the tiara from him and fixed it in her hair. "How does that look?"

"Fine. Can we go now?" Daphne tried to herd Peggy toward the door.

A door opened in front of them and Noah emerged, followed very closely by Detective Widmore. Noah wore a T-shirt and jogging shorts, but the detective was dressed in a crisp white blouse and beige pencil skirt. A leather belt accentuated her narrow waist and her hair hung down her back in flowing waves.

Daphne didn't miss the appraising look Detective Widmore gave her and Peggy. Daphne suddenly wished she hadn't tossed on the first clothes within reach after receiving Peggy's call. Her shorts and T-shirt seemed dowdy in comparison, but it was midnight, she reminded herself, and they were all lucky she'd remembered to put on a bra.

"Hi, Noah," Peggy exclaimed. "What are you doing here? Did you get arrested too?"

Noah hesitated. Glancing at the detective, he said, "It was just a misunderstanding. But Ellen straightened everything out."

Daphne's curiosity was piqued, but she couldn't gather the courage to ask, especially not in front of *Ellen,* who kept studying Noah like he was a chocolate cheesecake. She couldn't deny he looked good enough to eat in his workout clothes, but after their conversation earlier, she knew that would never happen.

*Which was what she had been arguing for, wasn't it?*

"What kind of misunderstanding?" Peggy asked. Daphne wanted to throw Peggy over her shoulder and carry her out of the station.

Noah hesitated again. He looked at Daphne and disappointment crossed his face. She tried to ignore it, but she suddenly felt as if he knew her worst secrets and disapproved. He *did* know her worst secrets. He'd known them all along. What had changed?

"Peggy, it doesn't matter. Let's just go," Daphne said, walking toward the door. She wasn't sure if Peggy was following her and she didn't really care. She'd had enough awkward situations with Noah tonight, and she wanted to leave before this one got any worse.

"You might not care, but I want to know," Peggy called after her. "Aren't you concerned about your friend?"

Daphne stopped with her hand on the exit door. Sure, she was concerned about her *friend*, but Noah had made it clear he no longer wanted to be her friend. It was on the tip of her tongue to say so, but the detective spoke first.

"It was nothing, really. Just a case of mistaken identity."

Daphne turned and waved to Peggy. "See? Hardly worth the question. Let's go."

"Actually," Detective Widmore said slowly, "I should probably give you a few more details since he was arrested at your house."

"My house?" Daphne returned to the group, looking from Noah to Detective Widmore and back again. "What were you doing there?"

Noah swallowed and cleared his throat. "I wanted to check out the shoes."

"Shoes?" She was beginning to wonder whether Peggy had slipped something into one of her drinks, because this was taking a right turn on the road to bizarre.

"I haven't had any luck running down Aaron Banks and I suspected he might show up at your residence sooner or later. I put a couple officers on a stakeout to watch for him. They saw Noah and he matched the description," Detective Widmore said nonchalantly.

*She could be nonchalant. She hadn't been under police surveillance.*

"Did you know about this?" Daphne asked Noah. This would be another thing friends should share. All the anger she'd nursed as she paced his driveway came rushing back. "And what's this about shoes?"

"I had to see if Aaron was telling the truth," he muttered.

"About what?"

"Being at your house. The fire. All of it."

"I told you he was at my house. How did you know about the fire?" Then it hit her. "You heard everything through the bathroom door, didn't you?"

Noah looked a little sick. "Not everything, but more than enough."

"Were you satisfied?" she snapped. She was starting to wonder if she really knew Noah at all. Eavesdropping, keeping secrets. It all seemed out of character to her.

"I got answers, but they weren't the ones I wanted to hear."

"Serves you right."

Detective Widmore smiled smugly.

"Is there anything else you'd like to tell me or should I wait until the SWAT team breaks down my door?"

Detective Widmore pursed her lips as if she was debating with herself. "We took Aaron's shoes into evidence. If you see or hear from him, please call me at once." She whisked a business card out of her pocket and handed it to Daphne. "It's very important we speak to him."

"I don't plan on seeing him." She ignored the outstretched card. Why would she need to call, when *Ellen* already had her house under surveillance?

"Just in case." Detective Widmore pushed the card toward her.

Daphne handled the card as if it might grow fangs and bite her. She tucked it into the pocket of her shorts.

"Let's go, Peggy." She reached for Peggy's arm to pull her down the hallway. Peggy seemed to be trembling. The irritated look on her face had changed to anger.

"How dare you insinuate anything about Daphne and Aaron?" The cup dropped from Peggy's hand, splashing hot coffee everywhere. Noah and Detective Widmore leaped backward. Noah's reflexes were quicker and he missed the brunt of the steaming splash, but the detective wasn't so lucky. Nor was her white shirt.

Now the detective was screeching.

"Like Daphne would ever invite him over. He's pond scum!" Peggy continued shouting. One hand made sure her tiara stayed firmly on her head, while the other jabbed a manicured finger at the detective. "He's lower than pond scum. He's the stuff under the squishy goo on the bottom of a pond."

"I'll get some paper towels," Noah said, dashing away from the scene.

Daphne threw the detective a quick glance. Her shirt was

definitely ruined and it looked like her skirt and peep-toe pumps had suffered the same fate. Daphne hid a smile. Peggy had just made up for all the horrors of her bachelorette party.

Noah returned with some damp towels, offering some to Peggy, who ignored his gesture and muttered about goo and bottom feeders. Detective Widmore blotted at the stain, then fled to the bathroom.

Noah wiped up the mess on the floor with the remaining towels. Peggy leaned against the wall, then slid to the floor. Her caffeine buzz must have worn off. She blinked bleary-eyed at Daphne.

Daphne bent to help Noah with some stray coffee splatters. He was close enough that Daphne could feel the warmth from his body. He didn't say anything and she didn't respond. What was there to say? The silence still felt awkward. She pulled Peggy to her feet and steered her toward the door. Detective Widmore emerged from the bathroom with the front of her clothing a wet, wrinkled mess. Daphne supposed she'd have to change and hoped the only extra clothing around here was an orange prison jumpsuit.

"See you later," Noah called.

Peggy harrumphed, but sauntered toward the door. Daphne held it open for her. As Peggy went through, Daphne heard Noah promise to take *Ellen* for coffee the following day. Daphne let go of the door. It didn't slam, but slowly closed. *So much for being his one and only,* she thought, retrieving her car keys from her pocket.

## Chapter Twenty-four

Daphne sipped her coffee, then swirled the straw around the ice chunks.

"What do you mean?" Beth asked. "I thought something might be starting between you and Noah. How can it be over? It's barely been a week."

Daphne swiped at the puddle of condensation from her glass with her napkin. After the disastrous bachelorette party and bailing Peggy out of jail the night before, Daphne had hoped she could cancel on Beth. But Beth wouldn't take no for an answer, especially after she'd heard bits and pieces of what had happened. The four tables in the coffee shop were already taken, so she and Beth sat at a café table on the deck. The sun was much too bright for four hours of sleep. Daphne dug in her purse for her sunglasses. She pushed them on her head, thankful for the protection from the sun and Beth's intense stare. "Whatever it was, it shouldn't have even started."

"But it did . . ." Beth prompted.

"And it's over." Daphne slouched in her chair and stared at the separating layers of water, coffee, and whipped cream in her glass.

"What happened? Something had to happen in order for whatever didn't start to be over." She mimicked Daphne's slouching posture.

Daphne jammed her straw against the ice chunks and wished she'd ordered a double shot of espresso. She needed it.

"I told him we should just stay friends." They weren't even close to friends. They were awkward strangers now.

Beth sucked air through her teeth, making a hissing sound. "I bet he didn't take that well."

"He said he had to fix me first."

*"Fix you first?"* Beth grimaced. "What the heck? When did he say that?"

"Last Sunday, when I was decorating your house." Daphne sipped her drink. "Jake wasn't too mad, was he?"

"He'll get over it, if you tell him how you stuck Jimmie Johnson to the ceiling."

Daphne half-smiled and shook her head. "Fat chance."

Grateful that Beth had taken her bait and followed the change of topic, Daphne was in safer waters. She really didn't want to talk about Noah or think about Noah or have Beth examine how she felt about Noah. She'd rather avoid Noah altogether. She tried to keep the conversation away from any of those topics.

"Did you hear about Peggy's bachelorette party?"

"She was arrested for assaulting a dancer and threw coffee on a detective," Beth said.

Daphne checked her watch. "I picked her up from the police station less than twelve hours ago. How'd you know all that?"

"Jake talked to Noah this morning."

"Huh." Daphne spooned a chunk of ice out of her drink and crunched it between her teeth.

"Speak of the devil." Beth waved to someone walking toward the café. Daphne turned to look and wished she hadn't. Noah stood on the sidewalk, scanning the tables.

Beth gestured for him to join them. Daphne kicked her shin, but Beth sent a glowing smile toward Noah. Daphne could see the instant he recognized Beth's companion. His step hitched and the smile on his face tightened.

"Good morning, ladies," he said, mostly to Beth. "How was your honeymoon?"

Beth's sigh turned into a grin. "Wonderful. Would you like to sit with us?"

Daphne kicked her shin again. Beth flinched and scowled at Daphne, but gestured to the open chair.

"I'd like to, but I'm meeting someone." He glanced at Daphne out of the corner of his eye.

"That's too bad," Beth said.

"Yeah, too bad," Daphne echoed, focusing on pleating her napkin into a fan and trying to hide her relief.

Having coffee with him would be more uncomfortable than cleaning up after Peggy last night was, with Beth evaluating every word and glance for an ulterior motive.

After checking the entrance, he said, "She's here. Catch you later."

*She?* Daphne snuck a peek at the doorway. Her jaw fell open.

"Detective Widmore?" she whispered, as if the name tasted like vinegar. "I knew she was after him."

"Who's she?" Beth asked, staring at the woman Noah escorted to a table on the other side of the café.

"That's Ellen."

Beth swiveled in her chair.

"Don't look at her," Daphne hissed.

"Business or pleasure? I wonder . . ." Beth mused.

"Does she look like she's dressed for business?" Daphne snapped.

Detective Widmore wore a cotton T-shirt and a short denim skirt. The V-neck of the T-shirt hinted at cleavage from across the room. Daphne was sure there was more than a hint from Noah's point of view.

Of the four coffee places in town, they had to pick this one. Daphne took a long drink from her coffee. The cold gave her an instant brain freeze, echoing the pain of seeing Noah with another woman.

Beth had turned completely around in her chair and was focused on Noah's table.

"Would you turn around?" Daphne hissed again. "You're drawing attention."

"Not theirs. Is she from around here?" Beth asked, righting herself in her seat.

"She's the detective who grilled me about setting the fire at the Willows. Noah told her I did it."

Beth glanced over her shoulder. "Noah wouldn't do that."

"How else would you explain it? She was ready to slap the cuffs on me."

"Perhaps she had an ulterior motive. I think she wanted to get you out of the picture."

Daphne arched her eyebrows and Beth continued. "Look how she's sitting with him. She's leaning toward him and twirling her hair. She's flirting." Beth laughed. "Wow, she's obvious. He doesn't seem to get it, though."

Daphne peered around Beth. Detective Widmore had chosen the seat directly to Noah's right instead of across from him. He leaned away from her, his arms crossed.

"He's got to be interested. Why else would he invite her to coffee?" Daphne asked. "He's probably feeding her more dirt on me now that he hates me."

Beth faced Daphne and cocked her head toward her. "Would you listen to yourself?"

Daphne returned her attention to her drink, avoiding Beth's scolding gaze.

"We're not in junior high anymore." Beth thumped her travel mug against the table.

Daphne flinched.

"And since you've turned Noah down, he can play the field if he wants. An attractive woman is interested in him. I say, why not go out for coffee?"

"Beth, you're supposed to be on my side."

"What is your side, Daphne? Do you even know? Because I thought it was that Noah was trying to pursue something you weren't interested in, but now it sounds like you are interested."

"I'm not."

Beth tilted her head to the side and pursed her lips. "Then why do you care who Noah is enjoying coffee with. You should be happy for him. He's probably your best friend."

"He was. After you, of course."

"That's right, you aren't speaking to him anymore."

"Maybe if it wasn't her. Noah knows how Detective Widmore treated me." She paused. "Actually, he doesn't know. I never got to tell him. Aaron showed up."

"What if it was someone else? Like that cute new math teacher."

Daphne shook her head. "She's too analytical for him. He needs someone more creative to keep him on his toes."

"So what's stopping you?"

Daphne looked across the café. Her reasons seemed ridiculous now. She wasn't confusing him with Aaron. She knew exactly who she was attracted to. She wouldn't lose a friend. She'd already lost him by not taking the risk.

"He's with her now." Daphne swirled her coffee. The murky brown suited her mood. "I'm too late."

"I wouldn't say that," Beth replied, as Daphne's phone rang.

Daphne fished her phone out of her handbag and checked the caller ID. She gasped. "Peggy! I forgot I was supposed to meet her to put together party favors for the reception. I better go."

## Chapter Twenty-five

Noah held Ellen's chair as she sat down. He still wasn't sure why he had invited her for coffee. Sure, she'd saved his behind last night, but meeting at the coffee shop felt strangely like a date.

And it felt like he was cheating. On Daphne.

*Why did Daphne have to be here this morning?* He sat down across from Ellen so his back was toward the table where Daphne and Beth sat. This way he wouldn't be tempted to look in their direction every few minutes.

Ellen grinned at him, then shaded her eyes. "Oh, the sun is bright here. I'll just switch seats." She scooted around the table so she was right next to him.

*So much for keeping some distance.*

"Sorry about the mix-up last night. Rookie officers don't like to be wrong," she said, tracing her finger along the mosaic design of the table. Her fingertips brushed along his arm. He slid it away.

"No harm done," Noah said, looking toward the kitchen and wondering when their coffees would be ready. *How long did it take to pour a cup of regular joe?*

"I'm glad. I was really surprised to see you last night. I thought maybe you'd come to the station for another reason." She pushed her hair over her shoulder. The flowing strands

172

dulled to white in the morning sun. Not like Daphne's, which shimmered gold.

"What reason would that be? You would have heard any first responder emergencies on the scanner." He decided to play obtuse. Maybe that would get him off the hook here.

"I thought maybe you had come to see me." She winked and inched her chair closer to him. He leaned away, trying to be casual about it.

"At midnight?" Obtuse wasn't going to do it.

"Stranger things have happened. So," she paused, "do you have any big plans for the Fourth of July? My brother has a place on a lake. They shoot fireworks. I'd love for you to come."

Noah held in his sigh of relief. He could dodge this one. "Actually, my friend is getting married that day. I'm in the wedding."

"Ooh. A tuxedo. I bet you'll look sexy, as usual. You'll have to show me pictures."

"I wish we were wearing tuxedos." Noah took his coffee from the server and was tempted to chug it. He'd suffer the burned tongue just to get out of here.

She accepted her coffee and took a dainty sip. "I don't think I've ever heard a guy say that."

"The couple that's getting married likes to go all out, and the wedding has a patriotic theme."

"That will be fun."

"You're not the one who has to dress like Uncle Sam." *Why did he tell her that?* He wasn't trying to prolong this conversation. Noah glanced at his pager. The red light glowed, telling him it was on. He thumbed the volume up. If there was a call, he didn't want to miss it. It would be the perfect excuse to leave.

"Uncle Sam? You've got to be kidding." She swatted his arm, then dragged her fingernails lightly over his skin.

"I wish I were." Out of the corner of his eye, he saw

Daphne hurry out of the café with her phone pressed to her ear. She stumbled over a chair and landed on the ground. She had righted herself and was out the door before he'd even had a chance to stand up. *Where's the fire?* he thought.

"That was graceful." Ellen laughed.

"I hope she's okay," Noah said, still looking at the door.

"As fast as she got up, she'd have to be." She took a sip of her coffee. "So are you going stag to this wedding?"

Noah saw the hook in that bait. "No, I'm escorting my mom."

"Oh. I'd love to meet her some time."

Noah took a long drink of his coffee, scouring his brain for something to talk about that didn't involve his dating life. "How's the, uh—"

The high-pitched tone emanating from his pager had never sounded so sweet. He yanked the black box off his belt and cranked the volume. He caught "structure fire" in between the scratches of static.

"I have to go. I'll see you around the station." He stood and headed for the exit, holding the pager close to his ear to hear the rest of the call.

Jumping in his truck, he flipped the switch for the emergency lights and sped out of the parking lot. The dispatcher broke through the static to give the address, but all Noah heard was the street name. He zipped through town and parked at the fire station. He was the first of the volunteers to arrive and hurried into his pants and boots. He swung his jacket over his shoulder and did a quick visual inspection of the fire engine before hopping into the driver's seat. His fellow volunteers climbed in behind him, one grabbing the radio and one opening the garage door.

Noah pressed the siren and navigated the engine through town, while his companion verified the address and relayed details of the fire from the dispatcher.

"Four-fifty-three Murphy Street," the man riding shotgun said.

Noah's brain stalled. The address. *Daphne's?*

"Fully engulfed. There may be someone inside," the radio operator shouted over the siren's wail.

"Damn," Noah muttered as he stomped on the gas. The engine whipped around the corner to Daphne's street. He could see the smoke rolling from the roof and he was sure it was her house. He raced through a thousand scenarios. Could she be in the house? Could she have gotten home this quickly? Maybe that's what her call was.

He scanned the street, but didn't see her Honda anywhere. He parked the fire truck at the curb in front of her house. First on the scene, he was in charge until the chief arrived. He directed the men to start setting up the hoses.

One of the officers who had arrested him the night before approached, as Noah swung his jacket over his shoulders and shoved his arms through the sleeves.

"We saw someone go around back and didn't see them again." Officer Baldus gestured toward the house. "We called headquarters because it looked like our guy, but we were waiting for confirmation on the license plate. Didn't want to make a mistake again," he said sheepishly. "We finally got confirmation, then we saw the smoke. I radioed dispatch and Officer Hopkins called the detective."

"Our guy? Aaron." Noah hooked the front of his coat together and grabbed his helmet from the seat.

"Yeah. Detective Widmore thought he might show up and wanted us to keep up the stakeout."

Noah surveyed the house. Smoke rolled out the kitchen windows and a separate plume oozed out the back of the house, but the flames seemed to be confined to the kitchen area.

"Either of you go in?" he asked.

Officer Baldus shook his head. "Officer Hopkins went to see if anyone was there. The slider on the deck was open, but we don't know for sure if anyone went inside. The suspect's car is still here." He pointed to the red Camaro parked down the block. The officer's radio rattled and he turned away from Noah. The chief pulled up and Noah briefed him quickly, then headed toward the house.

He kicked down the front door and a wave of smoke roiled out. Bending down below the smoke, he felt his way to the kitchen. Flames scarred the countertops and cupboards around the kitchen. He searched the floor, but found no one overcome by smoke. He quickly checked the living room and the bathroom. *Empty.* He headed for the bedroom. Then he heard the windows shatter and something smacked him in the back of the head.

## Chapter Twenty-six

Since you're late anyway, could you pick up some more red, white, and blue ribbon on your way over? I don't think we're going to have enough. We decided to put it on all the party favor bells for the tables, so they'll look like little Liberty Bells. Won't that be awesome?" Peggy squealed into the phone.

Everything for Peggy's wedding was red, white, and blue. They had red, white, and blue striped dresses and blue tuxedoes with starred vests and flags in their bouquets and boutonnieres. Thankfully, the theme had stopped short of the bridesmaids dressing as the Statue of Liberty with green hair and body paint to match their draping gowns. Daphne was careful not to mention anything of the sort to Peggy.

"Sure. No problem."

Daphne unlocked her car and tossed her purse across to the passenger side. She made the necessary errands as Peggy continued to call with requests for more things to pick up. Daphne had not been able to find the bald eagle statues at the hobby store, so she hoped that wasn't one of Peggy's favorite ideas.

She hefted the shopping bags into Peggy's house and dropped them on the counter. Peggy and the other bridesmaids huddled around the television.

"What's going on?" Daphne asked, as she moved to stand behind the sofa.

"There's a fire," Peggy said, barely turning from the screen. "Channel Four sent their helicopter out to cover it." Peggy pointed at the screen with the remote, thumbing the volume down. "Hey, I can hear it from here."

Daphne watched the smoke billow as the helicopter approached the fire on the screen.

"Channel Four always sensationalizes things. Somebody probably burnt their toast. Did they say where it is?" Daphne asked.

"They haven't given the address yet." Peggy cocked her head to the side as she studied the screen. "That looks familiar, though." The video cut away to a reporter and the fire chief. They were stationed in front of a fire truck, which obscured the view of the house. The reporter asked something and the fire chief shook his head.

"What's he saying?" Daphne asked.

Peggy raised the volume.

"You'll have to excuse me." The chief turned away from the reporter as another firefighter grabbed his arm.

The camera jerked up and refocused on the burning roof. Flames chewed away the side of the house as firefighters called for more hoses. Then the gabled roof tumbled into the center of the flames.

"Wow. That's scary. I'd hate to have been in there when that happened. I'd probably pee my pants," Peggy said, her eyes wide.

The camera panned backward, catching a glimpse of the house next door. Daphne jerked. *Her neighbor's.* "It's my house!" The words screeched out of her throat. She prayed they weren't correct.

As the shot grew wider, she had her answer. "My house is on fire," she said, as if she didn't understand the words. Her fingers clutched at the sofa.

"Holy crap!" Peggy exclaimed. "I've never known anyone whose house burned down."

Daphne buckled to her knees and pressed her chin against the coarse fabric of the couch. She could only whisper "My house is on fire" over and over.

The television cut to the reporter again. "Neighbors say they saw the smoke and called nine-one-one. There are conflicting reports about whether anyone was inside."

"Aren't you glad you were shopping for me?" Peggy said, patting Daphne on the shoulder. "I probably saved your life. You got me out of jail. I saved you from a fire. We're even, I guess."

Daphne jumped to her feet and headed for the door. "I've got to go."

"Hold on there," Peggy said, grabbing her arm. "You are in no condition to drive. Let me take you." Peggy snatched a ring of keys off a holder by the door and led Daphne to a vintage orange Volkswagen Beetle with flowers painted on it.

Daphne slid into the passenger seat and snapped her seatbelt as Peggy cranked the engine and jerked the little car out of the driveway. The tires spun on the gravel before catching the pavement. Peggy swerved around the first turn and Daphne clutched the door handle.

"My house may be on fire, but I do want to get there alive," she shouted to Peggy over the rattle of the engine, as the car rolled around another turn and Daphne was sure at least two wheels came off the ground.

Peggy slammed on the brakes at a stoplight and impatiently drummed the steering wheel. "I wish I had a siren," she muttered.

"Thank goodness you don't. The fire department is there. They're taking care of everything," Daphne whispered, trying to calm herself. Then another thought occurred to her. *What if*

*Noah was at the fire? What if something happened to him while he was trying to save her house?* The roof collapse had looked bad. *What if he was underneath it?*

Mind-numbing terror replaced the hysteria she'd felt before. She had to get to Noah. She couldn't live without seeing him again. He was her rock. The one person she depended on for everything. The one person she couldn't live without.

*Couldn't live without?*

Yes, it had been barely twenty-four hours since that awful incident in the parking lot, and she felt like the foundation of her life was broken. Her heart had a giant crack only Noah could repair.

*If he would forgive her, that is.*

The light changed and Peggy proceeded through the intersection at a grandmotherly pace.

Daphne reached across the car and pushed Peggy's knee down. "Pedal to the metal, lady. I have to see Noah."

Peggy readily complied, and the neighborhoods whizzed by until they met the police barrier at the end of Daphne's street. Daphne leapt out of the car before it had slowed to a stop, pushing her way through the crowd of gawkers and reporters. She climbed on the hood of Aaron's Camaro to see over the people.

The frenzy of activity she'd seen on the television had diminished. The roof over the kitchen had caved in, and scorch marks outlined a gaping hole in the exterior of the house. Firefighters meandered around the yard, moving hoses and occasionally spraying water on the ceiling and roof.

A firefighter and another man stumbled out the front door, both collapsing on the grass at the bottom of the steps.

Even in his bulky coat and helmet, Daphne recognized Noah's form. She jumped off the car and ran toward the prone figure.

Noah ripped off his helmet and chucked his face mask to the side. His face and hair were drenched in sweat. He shed his gloves and tossed them on the grass. He'd never looked so good.

The man beside him doubled over, coughing. His clothes were flecked with burn marks.

"There you are," a scratchy version of Aaron's voice said. "What'd you do with my shoes?"

Daphne ignored him and knelt beside Noah. He fumbled with the clasps on his jacket and Daphne pushed his hand away. She unhooked the clasps and shoved the heavy jacket off his shoulders.

"Are you all right?" she asked.

Two paramedics arrived before he could answer. One checked his vitals and handed him a bottle of water, while the other attended to Aaron. The paramedic tried to offer oxygen, but Noah pushed it away. Daphne's hand slid along Noah's arm until her fingers were entwined with his. Noah put the bottle of water to his mouth and, after taking a drink, splashed his face and hair. He shook his head and cool drops spattered onto Daphne, but she didn't move.

She tentatively touched his face. His damp hair. The prickly stubble already appearing on his chin.

"Noah, I'm so sorry." Cradling his hand to her chest, she said, "I didn't understand how I felt. It scared me."

Noah looked up at her. His blue eyes connected with hers. "Daphne, there was never anyone else for me. Only you."

He tossed the water bottle on the ground and cradled her cheek. She leaned into his hand, relishing the fevered warmth.

"I love you, Noah." She pressed her lips to his. "Do you still love me, even after all I've put you through the last few weeks?"

Detective Widmore walked across the grass toward them. *Why does she have to show up now,* Daphne thought.

"Oh please," a voice behind them whined. "Like Noah is some great catch." Aaron scrambled away from the EMT and threw his oxygen mask to the ground. "I'm glad I burned your kitchen. If I had knocked Noah out like I intended, the whole house would have gone up."

"You hit Noah?" Daphne asked, getting to her feet and grabbing Aaron's shirt. He tried to twist away, but she yanked him closer.

"He was wearing a helmet," Aaron said, attempting to untangle her fingers from his collar.

"Which is why the shoe didn't knock me out," Noah said, but Daphne didn't hear him.

She jammed her knuckles into Aaron's jaw so hard he lost his balance. She heard the satisfying crunch as his teeth smashed together. He stumbled to the grass, cradling the side of his face. Daphne shook her hand out, trying to get her joints back in their proper place.

Aaron swore. "You betrayed me. I'm glad I burned your house down."

"Sounds like a confession to me." Detective Widmore whisked handcuffs out of her rear pocket and onto Aaron's wrists. The move was so smooth and quick, Aaron seemed surprised at the constraints.

"What the—?" He shook his wrists. They were securely fastened behind his back.

"You're under arrest for arson." She listed the charges and then read him his rights. Grabbing his arm below the elbow, she hoisted him to his feet and pushed him toward a waiting squad car. Daphne thought she heard Aaron sobbing. "But it was an accident. I was just looking for my shoes."

"And that caused the kitchen to burst into flames how?" the detective asked.

"My shoes were gone, and then I found a detective's business card. I thought Daphne was going to turn me in. So I tried to burn the card on the stove. The towels on the oven handle caught fire and I panicked."

"You better hope that's what the evidence shows." The detective didn't miss a step.

"What about my shoes?" He jerked around to face Daphne. "She stole my shoes."

The detective glanced back at Daphne. "I took your shoes. Get in the car."

Daphne felt Noah's arms wrap around her.

"How's your hand?" he asked.

"Hurts like the dickens," Daphne said, flexing her fingers.

Noah gently lifted her hand and kissed each of the swollen knuckles. "I'll always love you, Daphne," he murmured in her ear. Then he kissed her lips with a heat that put her burned-out kitchen to shame.

## *Epilogue*

Daphne walked down the aisle cocooned in a red, white, and blue dress in the style of the Statue of Liberty. It draped over one shoulder, and the stripes were diagonal. Her bouquet consisted of red, white, and blue flowers intermingled with reflective streamers and tiny American flags. Thankfully, she and the other bridesmaids had talked Peggy out of the fireworks tiaras she'd found at a party store for—can you believe it?—a dollar each. Daphne did have a crown of patriotic carnations around the pile of curls on top of her head, though.

As with everything Peggy did, the wedding was over the top. Flags marked each row of chairs and waved from the rear of the limo on either side of the JUST MARRIED sign. There were probably fewer flags at a state dinner.

As all weddings held outside on a ninety-degree day should be, this wedding was short. The minister read the vows, and Peggy and Dustin lit a Roman candle. Moments later, they were marching back down the aisle to "God Bless the U.S.A."

Kisses and hugs were exchanged with the bride and groom as the guests trickled through the receiving line. Noah pulled Daphne out of the mob of congratulating guests as soon as there was a break. He pushed her toward a secluded arbor.

"All I could think about as we stood up there was how deep

your patriotism went," he whispered, trailing a finger along the neckline of her gown.

"You'll have to wait until after the fireworks to find out," Daphne flirted back.

Noah nuzzled her neck and kissed the shallow indent at the base of her throat. "I was hoping we could make some of our own."

"That could be arranged." Daphne sighed contentedly.

"Daphne! Daphne! Where are you? We've got to hand out sparklers!" Merry called. She winked when she saw Daphne and Noah. "Whenever you're ready."

"Duty calls." She kissed Noah quickly on the lips, but he held her for a longer, lingering kiss.

"Until later then." He let her go.

Daphne moved through the rest of the reception in a dream. She always knew where Noah was, and whenever she looked his way, he was looking at her. Later in the evening, she found herself collecting dollar bills and handing out candy bars again.

A welcome voice spoke close to her ear. "So are we ever going to do this?"

"Like this?" Daphne gestured to the festoons of balloons and buntings, the crowded dance floor, and the inebriated guests. "Not in a million years."

"Then how are we going to do it?" He traced a finger along the back of her neck.

"You, me, a beach, and not a bridesmaid in sight."

"I'll order the tickets."